FOREVER

thatcher

FOREVER 18 BOOK 4

USA Today Bestselling Author
Heather Young-Nichols

Forever Thatcher
Forever 18 Book 4
USA Today Bestselling Author
Heather Young-Nichols

heatheryoungnichols.com

Ransom

Booker

Dixon

Finding Love

Making Her Mine

Making Him Hers

Harbor Point

Love by the Slice

Love by the Mile

Love by the Rules

Gambling on Love

Highest Bidder

Highest Stakes

Highest Reward

Holiday Bites

All I Want

All of Me

The Fallout Series

Last Good Thing

Last First Kiss

Last Chance Love

With J.A. Hardt

Bound by Magic

With Amelia J. Matthews

Dirt on the Diamond

After Office Hours: Seducing the Professor

1

THATCHER

There were very few days that I wished I could cut off my own head and toss it in a garbage disposal.

Today was one of them.

I didn't think I'd ever had such a miserable pounding pain in my entire life. Nor had my stomach been so twisty, ready to empty all of the contents of my stomach at any moment.

Though there wasn't anything in there to empty.

"You become a lightweight?" Jamison McCall, my best friend and drummer for my band, asked. Our band. Whatever. He was the drummer for Forever 18 and I'd known him a long fucking time.

Jamison was the dirty-blond bad boy of Forever 18 too and I had no doubt that he could drink any of us under the table easily. It was that he was larger.

We were all roughly the same size, though some had a little more muscle. Not much but a little. Our builds were slightly different but nothing that would stand out.

"Fuck off," I said with a groan as I ran a hand over my face. "I drank more than you did last night."

"Nah. I don't think so." His voice had a tone to it that told me he was going to enjoy fucking with me. "I remember you having one Cosmo then switching to Shirley Temples all night."

I raised a middle finger at him from across the room.

I'd never had a Cosmo or Shirley Temple in my life and he knew it.

He and I had gone out last night. There'd been drinking and women and I hadn't blacked out. But I also hadn't drunk a gallon of water before I'd gone to bed to keep this from happening. I shuffled over to the refrigerator on the bus and pulled out a Gatorade. I'd be drinking those like they were water today, but they were better than water for a hangover in my experience. I also grabbed a bottle of Tylenol out of the cupboard over the fridge and took two, though wanted to take many more.

"Last I saw you, you were running off with that redhead," I said once I'd drained half the Gatorade and swallowed the pills. The sound of the bottle hitting the table turned my stomach.

A slow grin spread across his face. "Yeah. She was fun."

Now that our other bandmates, Lennox Weaver, Grayson Cook, and London Kerr, had all found themselves in relationships, it was just Jamison and me who went out.

Sure, the guys would come sometimes, but it was like going out with your grandparents at this point. Either they brought the girls—who we loved, but they weren't exactly conducive to rock-star partying—or they wanted to get back early to be with them.

That wasn't Jamison or me.

"Do you hear anything I'm saying to you, Thatcher?" His tone told me that he'd kept talking, but my brain hadn't heard a word. It had probably tuned him out for protection.

"Not at all."

"You're grumpy when you're hung-over."

"So are you," I countered.

"Good thing I don't get hung-over."

There wasn't a comeback for that because it was true and absolutely annoying. I hadn't seen Jamison hung-over since we were in high school. Maybe that was due to the amount he drank or maybe it was genetics. I didn't know, but it irritated the fuck out of me.

"Morning, fellas." Grayson slapped me on the shoulder, jarring my brain against my skull.

"Fuck," I muttered under my breath.

I'm never drinking that much again. No matter how much fun I'm having.

"What'd you two do last night?" Grayson grabbed a bottle of water then fell onto the couch at the front of the bus with his legs up on the seats. His feet almost touched Jamison. Almost. Grayson's dark hair had seen better days so clearly he hadn't brushed it yet or anything and he was still just in his boxers.

"The fact that I did a redhead," Jamison told him without any hesitation. "But Thatch had a couple of drinks then passed out."

I rolled my eyes then reminded myself not to do that again.

Every fucking thing hurt.

"I didn't pass out," I told him, but my voice wasn't so convincing.

The bus hit a bump that sent my stomach reeling, but I wasn't going to throw up. I refused. If for no other reason than to not give Jamie the satisfaction.

"Looks like a couple of days off will do you some good," Grayson said, It took me far too long to realize that he was talking to me.

Finally, I told him, "I think it'll do *all* of us some good."

Touring wasn't easy. I mean, it wasn't hard , but it was tedious and could make you go a little stir-crazy. Sometimes, we didn't even see the outdoors. It was bus to venue to bus to venue. Each of us tried to get out when we could, even if it was just to grab a cup of coffee.

It just didn't always work out that way.

"It's still crazy to me that we did a song for a soundtrack," Grayson continued. "Our music is going to be in a movie."

That was the reason we were getting a few days off. We'd quickly recorded a song for what was supposed to be the biggest movie of the summer. It'd been months ago, before Lilah—our stylist and now Grayson's girl—had even joined the tour, and there'd been a question as to whether or not the song would actually make it into the final cut. So, we forgot about it and moved on with the tour.

Well, it had, and now the movie was premiering in L.A. and we were going.

Our first movie premiere and our first song on a

soundtrack. Our record had gone gold recently and this summer was turning out to be a big one for the band. And for the band members who had seemingly found their other halves.

The soundtrack was already having unprecedented downloads with our song being among the most popular.

"I'm just happy to have a few days alone with my girl," Grayson added.

I scratched the back of my head, but even that was too much pressure. "Didn't you just have that? You went somewhere with beaches."

"Yeah." He nodded. "But I'll take all the days alone with her."

"I'm just that amazing." Lilah's voice brought all of our attention to her. Not a one of us had heard her get out of the bunk. Her chocolate-brown hair was pulled back and while she'd probably slept on it like that, it looked like the messiness of it was on purpose. When her hazel eyes fell on me, she winced. "You don't look so good. Need me to get Avalon?"

I groaned. This was how the day was going to be.

Avalon was Jamison's sister and Lennox's new girlfriend. They'd recently gotten together when Avalon had come to visit her brother, but apparently, that shit had been brewing for years. She was also an

EMT. Hence the reason why Lilah had asked if I needed her.

"I'm fine," I told her.

She snorted, like she didn't believe a word out of my mouth. "You need some greasy food."

My stomach cramped at the thought of food, but she was right. A nice, greasy breakfast was exactly what I needed.

Lilah didn't wait for a response before she headed up to the front, giving Grayson a quick kiss on her way past, and pulled the little slider back. She spoke to the driver quietly, or at least I couldn't hear her over the pounding in my head. Then she was back with her hands on her hips.

"I'm going to wake everyone up to see if they want breakfast," she told us. "We've got a couple more hours before our flight to L.A., so he's finding us someplace to eat that isn't too far from the airport."

Lilah breezed past me again and began knocking next to the bunks. The knocking I could've done without.

We'd only left our last arena this morning. We were supposed to drive to Atlanta to catch a flight. Our show had been a little out of the way last night. The nearest airport was tiny and didn't have any flights that would work. So we were driving two hours to catch a flight and were probably almost there.

But fifteen minutes later, the entire group of us were stepping off the bus at an IHOP.

We were a large group, given that it was Jamison; Lilah's assistant, Becca; Grayson and Lilah; London and Charlotte; Lennox and Avalon; and me. But the hostess was more than happy to accommodate us. It only took them a couple of minutes before they had the tables pulled together so that we could all sit together.

What surprised me was when a few minutes later, Sean walked in.

Sean Caspian was a big guy and our manager. Tall like the rest of us with a lot more muscles. He had dark-blond hair and eyes so dark, it felt like he could see into your soul.

It shouldn't have surprised any of us that he'd shown up. His bus would've been traveling with ours since he was supposed to be on the same flight.

"You don't look so good," Sean said, clapping me on the back roughly.

"People keep saying that and I'm going to get a complex." I had brown hair that I kept short with a kind of faux hawk thing at the front and brown eyes, but more than one person had told me that I was above average in many departments, but specifically attractiveness.

Now I didn't go around thinking about whether I was hot or not, but all of a sudden, everyone wanted to tell me that I looked awful. It was the hangover. I knew that.

But fuck. Give a guy a break.

"Please." Sean snorted. "You're the guy every woman wants to take home to Mom and Dad."

I shook my head because that couldn't have been further from the truth and I didn't want it to be true anyway.

I had tattoos down both my arms that moms and dads usually didn't love. Sure, cleaned up and wearing the right clothes, I could've looked like every parent's dream come true. But change any of that and I'd never met a parent happy to discover that I was seeing their daughter.

Which was why it was best to avoid the hassle, unless you couldn't.

"I need carbs," I said to no one in particular. So when the waitress appeared, I ordered a stack of pancakes with a side of bacon.

"What's the clothes situation?" Sean asked Lilah after we'd all ordered.

The hostess was bringing out the drinks we'd ordered before the waitress had taken our food order. I had just wanted good old black coffee.

"Suits were delivered to the office a few days ago," Lilah responded. "So they should all be set."

"Good." Sean took a drink of his coffee. "And you all are good too?"

She smiled widely. "Sean." Then she shook her head. "We're the queens of shopping. I even ordered something for Avalon and it's there already."

He nodded.

This was a big deal. We were all going to be dressing the part. Now, the guys' and my suits didn't match like we were a boyband, but they were all dark suits appropriate for the event. At least according to Lilah.

I'd have to trust her on that.

It was also going to be the first event where three of our members had girlfriends along with them. So that was going to be out there on the Internet for all to see, though they weren't going to the premiere, walking the red carpet, or any of that bullshit. The guys were bringing their girls to the afterparty. At least the women didn't seem to mind and understood that there would be times that we had to be a band. Like for the red carpet.

They didn't care. They had each other to pass the time with.

It surprised me that Avalon had come back on tour with Lennox once he'd gone home to win her back. I would've thought she'd stay there and get back to work. She was a stickler about her work. But no. He'd come back with her on his arm and the only thing I knew was that she'd be staying for the rest of the summer. They'd reevaluate after that since she was hoping to start school in the fall.

We were going to Europe once our US tour was done, but that was for the couples to figure out and it was only for a couple of weeks. Just a few shows, nothing huge.

My pancakes arrived and I lathered those babies with butter and syrup then dove in.

They melted in my mouth and I couldn't get enough.

Lilah had been right. It was exactly what I'd needed.

Once everyone was finished with their breakfasts, we piled back onto the bus to head to the airport. Though this time, the place was Crazy Town. Everyone was trying to get their things packed, though not everything because we'd be back on this bus in a few days.

Sean had told us that the buses were going to be stored in Atlanta and the drivers were going to do whatever the fuck they wanted. But would meet us back here in time to get back on the road again.

Security ushered us through the airport, which was weird. We just needed to hurry and I guess that was Sean's solution, but having security do that actually brought more attention. Not less.

People watched as the group of us pushed through the crowds, some wondering who we were though I heard several yelps and say they needed their camera. There was no time to stop for pictures.

But whatever. We were through and boarding very quickly.

Now I was on my way home or at least the home away from home to a place that still didn't feel like home with a raging fucking headache that was just now beginning to subside to go to a fucking party that I didn't want to go to.

Tomorrow was going to be fucking fantastic.

2

MODESTIE

"I just spent six years being the chosen one," I told my agent, Brian, though I wanted to throw my phone through the window.

I shouldn't have to explain this to him, but at a time I thought he'd be listening to me more, he'd started listening to me less and less. Which was annoying, considering that he used to only listen to my father. Now that I was an adult, he had no one else to run to when he wanted me to behave.

"Modestie." He sighed while I cringed at the way he pronounced my name.

The mispronunciation was, in part, due to me being French. Though I no longer spoke with a heavy French accent, unless actually speaking the language, I'd been born and raised there, but now, it was only slight most of the time.

He pronounced it *modesty*, as in *he should understand I'd like to keep some of my modesty.* When really, my parents had pronounced it *mode-est-y.* As in, *my fucking name is Modestie.*

"No, Brian. I told you. I don't want to do any YA fantasy book series adaptions. Not for a while. Maybe not ever." OK. Maybe my accent came back a bit when I was angry because right now, I very much sounded like a French girl.

"This could be a big one," he countered.

I pinched the bridge of my nose and sighed. What he meant was it could be a big check, which in turn would mean that he would get a big share.

"No," I said with more finality. "I spent six years, actually seven because of the one year we didn't film, being the chosen one in the Gassar series. The only one who could bring down the Republic. I'm done with that for now. I need something more grown-up. I need to make the crossover."

"But Modesty... You look like a teenager. You could pass."

"Maybe if you'd learn how to pronounce my name, I'd take you more seriously. For now, it's still a *no.* I'm not even going to read the script. I want more grown-up parts. Maybe a rom com. Something. And it's your job to make this happen. If I don't get paid, you don't get paid, and I'm not taking any parts just so that you get paid." I swallowed hard.

Throwing my *star power* around wasn't something that I liked to do, mostly because I didn't feel like I had any.

Most of my teen years had been spent with people telling me where to be and what to do. I'd just delivered the lines. Sure, I'd delivered them in a way that made grown men cry, but still. I had no part in the choices that had gotten me there. That girl was left in the past and I wasn't going back.

"Well, there's still the offer from Anison Brecht."

I cringed. Visibly. If he'd been in the room with me, he would've seen it. "No." My answer was immediate and firm. That wasn't a director I ever wanted to work with. "I'm not showing my tits for the world to see. No nudity."

Brian groaned. "Then I don't know what to tell you. These are the scripts that have hit my desk. Or at least the ones that I think are worthy."

Yeah. Right. He meant the ones that would get him paid the most.

Many people who don't understand the business would tell me to get rid of Brian and trust me when I say, I wish it was that easy. He had connections for days. He could get me the scripts and auditions for the parts I wanted, but it was only recently, after a well-deserved break, that I'd come back with my own ideas of the types of roles I wanted to play.

Plus, the more he wanted to get paid, the harder he'd work. Or that was the theory that he hadn't yet proven.

Now, he just needed to get with the program or, in the end, I would fire him even if it meant going with someone who wasn't as well-connected as he was.

"Brian," I said to capture his attention. "I don't want to do nudity and I want grown-up parts. I'm twenty-three years old, for Christ's sake. Yes, I can play younger. Older would be a bit harder because I do look so young, but for fuck's sake, start getting me scripts that have a chance." I took a breath as an idea came to me. "Better yet, I'd like to see the scripts that have been sent to you that you've rejected. I'd like to look at them myself."

"Modestie, I don't think—"

"I don't care what you think. I want them. Send them to me." I held the line while my heart began to race.

This was the first time I'd really put my foot down with him.

I'd come back to acting six months ago after taking some time off and so far had only done a few smaller parts. Now I wanted more.

When I'd been fifteen, I'd gotten the part of Araya, the only one who could bring down the Republic of Gassar. It was a dystopian fantasy type situation and I'd loved doing it. At first. Then the hours had gotten long, the shoots even longer. I'd left school and got a tutor. Then, when I'd been seventeen, I'd demanded to actually go to school for my last year. More than that, I'd decided I wanted to do an exchange program to get away from my father, Brian, and all of the pressures.

My father had been furious. How dare I alter the plans of the producers of the Gassar Empire? It didn't matter. The last movie we'd shot was going to need such a long time for CGI that the producers had agreed it had been a good time for a break. A break would build the fandom's excitement, they'd said.

So I'd gone to Michigan with a student exchange program for my last year of high school and it had been the best of my teen years. I hadn't chosen Michigan. That was where I'd been placed and I had an amazing host family. Of course their kids were huge fans of the Gassar books and the movies but they quickly got used to me being there.

Then it had been back to work. The series had ended with the last release a year and a half ago. Which was when I'd taken another year off, which I'd spent traveling and removing my father from most aspects of my life.

Everyone had heard of stage moms, but mine was a stage dad and I wasn't sure which was worse.

But I loved acting and now it was time to get back to work.

"Brian?" I asked when he hadn't answered.

"I'll have them sent over," he agreed reluctantly. "But I'm telling you. Most of them are shit."

"We'll see."

I ended the call knowing that most of the scripts probably were shit. Most of them were, but right now, I didn't trust Brian's judgement on that. He'd acted like the year he'd gone without new revenue streams due to me taking a sabbatical had left him in government food lines.

He had other clients.

He had other paydays.

I just happened to be the biggest, considering that my role as Araya had garnered me every nomination for every award it possibly could have. I'd been nineteen and the limelight had been extremely bright.

Not winning any of those awards had been crushing. It had been part of what had led me to take the year off once The Gassar Saga had ended. That and I had been tired of all my firsts happening in front of a camera.

My first kiss. My first love scene, even if it had been pretend and not explicit, had been impossibly embarrassing. Not so for my costar, since he'd been a few years older and a few hundred years more experienced. At least he was one of the nicest guys that I knew and he'd been extremely careful as well as patient with me. He'd make sure I was OK with everything that was going to happen and if I wasn't, he'd take the blame for it.

I still love that guy.

Now, I wanted to move on. I'd be forever grateful to everyone who'd put me in the position to play Araya, but I wanted to prove that I could do more than her. Different characters. Different types of movies.

"Is he going to send the scripts?" Margot asked after I hadn't noticed she'd entered my hotel room. Or suite. Whatever. She always reserved me something spacious where she and I could get work done, but also, I could feel comfortable when there was down time.

It wasn't like money was an issue. I'd been the highest paid child actor in any series ever and of all the bad things I could've said about my father at a moment's notice, negotiating contracts wasn't one of them. I'd come out of that series with nearly a hundred million dollars.

I shrugged. "I hope so. He's walking a fine line and doesn't even know it."

Margot nodded as she set her iPad on the table near the couch. Her hair flowed over her shoulders in all of its purple glory. Margot looked more like a rock star than the personal assistant she'd been for the last three years.

Her hair had been dirty blonde at one point, I was told, but since I'd known her, she'd kept the purple. It was a subtle purple, not overpowering, and looked more lilac than anything else. She also had a full-sleeve tattoo running down her right arm and just looked like a badass in general.

I'd considered getting a tattoo once. My father had freaked out and told me that it would ruin me for any parts I may want. That had been enough to scare me off.

"I wish he'd cross that line," she mumbled, bringing a smile to my face.

There was no love lost between Margot and Brian.

"I really don't want to have to find another agent right now," I said. She raised an eyebrow at me. "But I will if I have to."

"He's just so…"

"Dismissive? Condescending? Still treats me like I'm the fifteen-year-old girl stepping on a set for the first time?"

"Yes. All of that."

Brian and my father had become friends before I started acting, though I had no idea how, and he'd been my agent since the beginning. It was like he and my father had gone into a room and plotted out my life and now both of them were upset that I've taken over and wasn't following their plan.

"Your father called," she said, interrupting my thoughts with the news that I always hated to get.

"And?"

"I told him I'd pass along his message." She swallowed then wet her lips. There was also no love lost between her and my father, either. "He wants to know when you're going to come to your senses and take a meeting with Anison Brecht."

I groaned as I threw myself onto the couch. "Never. And I've told him that."

She sat down more gently. "He knows. He's just upset you're not letting him dictate your life and probably kind of pissed that you have me answering the only number he has for you."

I snickered. That probably *was* pissing him off.

"But," she continued, "*baise-le.*" Which made me cackle.

Margot hadn't learned much French since taking this job, despite her giving it her best shot. But the swear words... Those she'd picked up quickly.

"Yes," I told her. "*Baise-le. Baise les deux.*" And I meant it.

Once our giggles had settled down, Margot flipped open her laptop. "Now, onto our work, which doesn't include the stupid men in your life."

I hopped up to grab a bottle of water out of the minifridge. Once I got my own place in California, I'd be a lot happier. Having my own space meant everything to me. If I was going to be serious about acting, I'd need a place here, even if I didn't make it my permanent residence. Because my gorgeous flat in Paris would always be home base. Or that was the plan.

"Right. The reason we're in California."

"I have a realtor looking for places with your must-haves," she began. And honestly, I thought that Margot would be relieved once I had a place here too. Sure, she'd be the one taking care of it when I wasn't here, but it'd be a home base for the two of us since she worked from California and sometimes came to Paris to meet with me. "He thinks he can have a short list of places in a couple of days."

"We'll be looking at them, right?"

"Of course." She scrunched up her eyebrows, as if she didn't understand why I'd be asking. "I'll probably look at them first to make sure they're worth your time, unless you want to see them all."

"No." I shook my head. "That's fine. You know what I like better than I do."

"Damn right." She glanced down at her iPad for the next thing. "You have the premiere tonight and your dress options are in the bedroom already."

I groaned. Premieres weren't my favorite. Too many lights, too many people all asking the same questions and even after several years, they will all be about playing Araya or asking what I was up to now.

The former, I'd already answered every question there was. The latter... I had nothing to answer with.

"That's right," I told her. "I remember. You're going with me, right?"

She nodded. "I have a beautiful yet utilitarian dress already chosen. I'm not wearing heels, though, because of all the running and I fucking hate them."

"You know I don't care what you wear."

She sat back with a sigh. "I do know, but I need to look the part. Plus, I look amazing in this dress."

I was sure she did.

Margot was beautiful. She was only slightly taller than I was, maybe five-foot-four inches or so. A little curvier than me, but I knew grown men who didn't want to mess with her. She was protective of her space and of me. It was like having a personal assistant and bodyguard all in one. Perfect for when I didn't have an actual bodyguard with me.

I hated having to hire them and only did it when necessary. Bodyguards drew attention which was the last thing I wanted most of the time.

"Also..." She trailed off the way she did when I wasn't going to like what she had to say.

"What? Margot, what?" My anxiety inched up when she did that, though I'd never told her.

"According to *Brian*"—she said his name as if it were sour on her tongue—"you need to go to the afterparty."

I furrowed my brows. That shouldn't be something she wouldn't want to address. "I figured. I usually do. It's when all the schmoozing happens."

"Well…" She swallowed hard. "The afterparty is hosted by Anison Brecht. They guy dying to see your tits on screen."

Groaning as I fell against the back of the couch, I searched my brain for every excuse I'd ever thought of to get out of it.

I'd auditioned for him once and he'd insisted I do something that I hadn't been totally comfortable with and now he did seem rather obsessed at the idea of getting me naked on screen. It was the reason that I made a point to never be where he was. No one knew about the audition, as it had been just him and me in the room. My father and Brian knew the audition was happening but not what occurred inside.

No matter how many times they grilled me about why I hadn't gotten the part, I never told them.

But if I wanted a serious career, I needed to do this.

Though resting on my laurels and the massive amount of money I'd made from Gassar was looking better by the day.

"I have to go," I told her, though the lack of excitement in my voice wouldn't go unnoticed.

"I know. I'll be there, too." She wrapped an arm around me for comfort. "You really need to tell me why we hate that guy so much."

The fact that she'd said "we" brought a small smile to my face.

Margot always had my back.

"Maybe one day," I told her with no intention of ever following through. "But for now, maybe there'll be a knight in shining armor at the party and I won't have to deal with Brecht."

There wouldn't be. But I'd find someone to attach myself to so that I wouldn't have to face the worst person I'd ever met all alone.

3

THATCHER

"Fuck," I muttered as I pulled at the tie around my neck. "Do people really think rock stars dress like this?"

Lilah rolled her eyes as she came over to tighten my tie again. "Don't be such a bitch. You're all providing a united front and this is a good look. You've worn suits before."

Yeah. We had. But for some reason today, I felt like I was being tied up in a straitjacket. Maybe it was leftover hangover from the day before.

"Yeah, but I feel like you ordered these extra snug." I pulled at the crotch of my pants to prove the point.

"Yeah, yeah." She sighed and lightly slapped my shoulder. "You have a big dick, we get it." Lilah couldn't have sounded more bored and I couldn't help but laugh.

"Yet you never prove it." Her best friend, Becca, piped up from the other side of the room. Becca was another pint sized woman on the road, though she wasn't attached to any of us. She was Lilah's best friend and assistant, but she didn't blink twice over giving each one of us shit especially when we deserved it. She had her long blonde curls pulled back in a ponytail as her brown eyes roamed over each of us, making sure that we looked exactly how we were supposed to.

Becca might joke about seeing our dicks but she one hundred percent didn't want to see a single one of them. She liked men. Just not any of us and that was perfect. There was no jealousy with the girl-friends, and no weirdness with the guys.

The five of us were getting ready at Grayson's house to make it easier for Lilah. Though it was like she and Becca didn't think that we could get dressed separately and still make it on time. I had to cut her some slack when it came to this since this was a band event. It made sense, but fuck, my tie was tight.

"Can you at least leave me some room to breathe?"

"If you're lucky," Lilah told me, then she turned

her attention to the other guys. "Looks like you're all ready."

Our suits were all dark but not exactly the same color. Yet no one would be able to say that any one of us looked out of place.

"The girls and I are meeting you at the after-party, right?" Lilah asked, but it took looking at her to see that she was talking to Grayson.

I knew she wasn't talking to me because I had no fucking clue what the women were doing, other than they weren't going to the premiere with us because it was basically a press event.

"Yeah," Gray confirmed. "The car will be here at eight and already has the address." He leaned down to kiss her softly on the lips, which was my cue to turn away.

I was glad Grayson had found his person and if I was being honest, I knew that they'd be together forever. He wasn't going to do anything to jeopardize his relationship the way Lennox almost had with his. But that didn't mean I wanted to *watch* that kind of tenderness.

And I wouldn't be delving into why that was the case.

The five of us and Sean piled into a huge SUV and were headed to the premiere. Lennox was the definition of panty-dropping. More than one woman had said it. My guess was that the combination of dark hair with blue eye were too much to resist. London had the dark hair too though none of us with dark hair were exactly the same shade and I'd heard it said that his hazel eyes could melt a woman on sight.

I didn't know about any of that because I'd looked at them for years and hadn't melted. My panties had also stayed easily in place.

This was all exciting, but I also couldn't wait until it was over. Red carpet and all of that shit wasn't exactly the vibe of our band, but none of us could deny that this was a huge break for us.

"Everybody ready?" Sean asked once the SUV had stopped at the theater.

There was a crowd of people across the street that we could hear from inside the car. They were screaming names and clapping. Big fucking stars were supposed to be here and then there was us. The fact that we were pretty big fucking stars still hadn't set in with us because we just felt like those guys from Saginaw.

"Ready," I confirmed with the rest of the guys.

We stepped out to a swell of noise from the crowd. Someone called my name. Others were calling out the other guys' names. We waved and smiled, walking the red carpet, stopping for pictures when we were told to.

There was a woman, tall with brown hair pulled back into a ponytail and a headset over one ear, herding us through. She was the one to tell us to stop. Then we'd answer a few questions and were off for the next set of pictures. It was pretty quick.

We were about to head into the theater when the roar of the crowd grew and I knew someone big had just stepped out.

"Is that...?" Lennox trailed off as he leaned to look down the red carpet, which caused the rest of us to do it too.

"Shit," London muttered. "It is. I haven't seen her since senior year."

"Me, either," Grayson agreed.

But I couldn't stop staring.

Modestie Dubois was coming down the carpet much like we just had. She smiled and waved to the fans across the street, but I couldn't take my damn eyes off her.

The sun shined off her dark-blonde hair with the golden hue. I'd never seen a hair color quite like hers in my life. Her creamy skin looked so fucking soft as she glided from one spot to the next. The red lipstick framing her smile gave me some other thoughts. Thoughts I wasn't supposed to have because we were friends.

Her light pink dress was flowy and deep cut so that the area between her breasts was there for me to feast on. When she turned for the pictures of her dress, her dress also left most of her back open. It wrapped around her neck and her waist.

Modestie had always been beautiful, but not seeing her in person for a long time meant that I didn't know just how fucking breathtaking she'd become.

"What about you, Hatch?" London asked, using the nickname my older brothers had given me with the explanation that I'd hatched from an egg.

"What?" I asked because I had no idea what they were talking about. Forcing my eyes off of Modestie, I focused on London. It was the only way I'd have a chance of understanding him.

"Have you seen her since high school?"

I shook my head. "We texted for a while after she went back to France, but I haven't talked to her in years."

"She's fucking hot," Jamison offered, making my jaw clench. "I mean she was in high school, but now?" He made a noise in the back of his throat that made me want to rip his fucking head off. "You sure you didn't hit that back then?"

I shook my head. "We were friends."

He raised his eyebrows like he didn't believe me because he had good instincts, but I couldn't give a fuck.

No one knew what had happened between Modestie and me the night before she'd gone home and it was going to stay that way.

The closer to us she got, the more I couldn't take my eyes off her.

"Time to go in," Sean said as he herded us through the door.

The movie was good with a decent amount of action. Or I thought it was. It was hard to focus on when I knew she was in here somewhere and I was desperate to talk to her. To see how she was doing. Before I knew it, the audience was clapping, which meant the movie was over and it was time to head to the afterparty.

There were too many people at the theater for me to find Modestie and even if I had, was this the kind of place where I wanted to reconnect? Not really. But I also didn't want to miss my only fucking chance.

"She'll be at the afterparty, I'm sure," Jamison said once we were back in our SUV.

"Who?" I asked because he'd clearly been talking to me.

"Modestie. That was who you were breaking your neck to see, right?"

"I wasn't doing any of that," I countered.

"The fuck you weren't. And I don't blame you. That woman is hot as hell."

I groaned and rubbed my temple. "Can you not talk about her like that?"

He gave me a cocky grin. "Why's that? You got something to tell us? Am I going to lose my last fucking single man in this whole fucking group? I mean I can handle all the groupies myself—we all know I can—but the question is, do I want to?"

"Yes," Grayson, Lennox, and London all said at the same time, making both Jamison and me chuckle. They weren't wrong. Jamison would love the challenge.

"You got me there," Jamison told them. "But if I have to see that fucker"—he stretched an arm out to point at Lennox—"with my own fucking sister, then you can handle me saying that the woman you've had a hard on for years for is hot as fuck."

I shook my head. "She's a friend."

"Keep telling yourself that," he countered. "Pretty soon, all you fuckers are going to have kids running around and wives and I'm going to be over here living my best life without any of you."

"Until you find the one," Lennox told him.

He waved his hand in the air. "Fuck all of that. There's no *the one* bullshit happening over here."

"Hang on." I cut in. "Why are you acting like I'm fucking off in a relationship? I'm not doing that bullshit right now, either. Eventually? Yeah, I think I'd like to have someone like that. Married? I don't know, but I'm still free as fuck right now."

Jamison chuckled. "The fuck you are. We all saw the way you were looking at her."

"I was just surprised to see her. You all don't know shit."

Luckily, they moved on quickly. Their attentions spans tended to be short.

Had my brain shorted slightly when I'd seen Modestie for the first time in years? Of course it had.

Was she beautiful? Absolutely.

Were we just friends who hadn't talked in a long time? Yes.

I also made a point not to stay up to date on any news about her, at least since the Gassar Saga had ended. I'd gone to see every single one of those movies and they were good movies on their own, but once Modestie had left Michigan, it had been the only way for me to see her.

We arrived at this upscale hotel where the after-party was being held. We were ushered in and greeted the movie's director and spent time chatting with a few of the stars. It was surreal. The place was already full, even though this ballroom had to hold a fair number of people.

The entire time, I kept an eye out for Modestie without looking like I was. Sean left after the premiere, as he didn't seem to think we'd need to be managed at a party. If there was one thing Forever 18 could do, it was party. Though this wasn't the kind we were used to.

People told us that they loved our song on the soundtrack. A few of the celebrities said they'd seen us live, though with the Hollywood crowd, you never knew if they were telling the truth or not.

Somehow I knew when Modestie had arrived. It was almost like a disturbance in the Force. Whispers and gossip filled the room. I hadn't seen her yet, but I knew she was there.

Still, it was more than an hour later before I actually saw her.

When she'd been in Michigan, she had already

been a star. Two of the Gassar movies had released and had been huge hits. Made a shit ton of money, if I remembered correctly. After a couple of weeks, most of the people in our school kind of forgot that she was a big star. Either that or they just got used to it and treated her like the rest of us.

Except a few of the guys. They'd wanted in her pants desperately and had been relentless. She'd rebuffed every single one, telling me that she wasn't interested in any of them, but that didn't mean they'd stopped trying. There'd even been a rumor she was seeing her costar but she adamantly denied that shit. He was older than her and honestly, that kind of thing could've brought shit down on his head. She hadn't turned eighteen yet.

As Modestie and I had become good friends, I'd made sure to run interference with all of those guys. If she didn't want them, then they were going to get the picture and high school boys are fucking idiots who don't like to admit defeat.

A couple of times Jamison and I had made sure they'd understood defeat.

Now, here in Los Angeles, that same girl, now a woman, was backed into a corner with a man I recognized but couldn't quite put my finger on who he was, crowding her fucking space.

She had a drink in her hand, clenched closely to her chest, as if she either didn't want to spill the liquid or she was using the drink to protect her like a shield he hopefully wouldn't penetrate. Her other arm was wrapped around her with her hand cradling her elbow.

It was like she was trying to make herself small when she was already small enough.

Fuck that. I wasn't going to sit here and watch her squirm because right then, she was.

The fucker reached out and trailed his fingers down her bare arm, causing her muscles to tighten.

What the fuck was he thinking?

He was probably five-ten, a few inches shorter than I was, definitely smaller than me in every other way as well, but Modestie was only like five-two or three. With the heels, maybe five-five, and he was looming over her like he was the predator and she was his prey.

When she swallowed hard, I didn't need to convince myself to step in.

I'd do this for anyone, but with Modestie, it was different.

I'd kept the creepy fuckers away from her the year she'd gone to our school and I'd do it again.

With zero fucks about who this guy was or what he could do to my career, if anything.

All that mattered in the moment was the Modestie was uncomfortable and I wasn't going to let that continue.

No matter what I had to do.

4

MODESTIE

I should've known better than to come to this afterparty alone and not wait for Margot when she'd gotten delayed. Silly me thinking that being around a hundred or more people would mean that those I didn't wish to speak to would stay far, far away.

If Margot had been here, she'd have given him a verbal smackdown that would have left him feeling about an inch tall before he'd ever gotten a word out.

Right now, I craved that. On the other hand, I still wanted to work in this business.

"Modestie," Anison Brecht said as he came toward me. "I was hoping I'd see you tonight."

Of course he was, especially since he was the one person I never wanted to see.

Anison was tall and attractive by anyone's standards. Even into his forties, he'd kept the look of an art school student and I didn't know if that was to make him more desirable to young women or if that was just how he liked it.

His blond hair would've fallen over one eye if he didn't have it tamed into submission with who-knew-how-much product. His blue eyes sparkled, like he always knew a secret you didn't. Anison had the all-American high school football quarterback look about him with just a touch of nerd. Most people wouldn't suspect a thing negative about him because to most, he was utterly charismatic.

To me, he looked like the one of the zombies from a horror movie because his personality had decayed long ago.

"Anison." My greeting was cold—cool at least. As he stepped toward me, I stepped back.

"It's been a while." He leaned in to kiss my cheek, but I snapped my head away from him.

There was nothing that would change the fact that this was the man I'd auditioned for when I'd been seventeen and hoping to work with one of the biggest directors in the industry while also breaking out of the Araya from Gassar typecasting.

It'd been a stretch, but I'd wanted it so badly.

"Has it?" I asked so that he'd know that I hadn't

thought of him for a second since the last time I'd seen him. Well, I had. But not for the reasons he probably hoped.

"It has." He gave me that all-too-confident grin of his, then took a drink of his cocktail. I had no doubt there was alcohol in that drink. With Anison, there always was. "Listen, I've talked to Brian a few times and sent over a script for my next project. He says you won't even consider it."

I swallowed hard and clutched the cool glass in my fingers. "It's just not the kind of project I'm looking for right now."

He cocked his head to the side and looked at me like I was a child being obstinate. I couldn't believe this shit worked for him with other actresses.

"It's going to be big, Modestie." At least he had the courtesy to pronounce my name correctly. Brian seemed to be the only one who had an issue with it and for a long time now, I thought it was on purpose.

"I'm sure it will be. It's just not what I'm looking for."

"Have you read the script?" He raised his eyebrow at me. My years of acting made it possible for me to hide the way he was making me feel.

This man was pushing me. He knew damn well that I hadn't read the script and why I didn't want to work with him. He also knew that I couldn't say that, especially at a party where anyone could overhear me. My heart was beating hard against my chest and my muscles were tense in preparation for fight-or-flight. Because that was what I was feeling. Fight. Or Flight.

I wanted to flight.

"I don't need to," I told him honestly as I took another step away from him. "Brian explained all that the part entails and it's not something I'm interested in. Honestly, I shouldn't have to explain why."

His blue eyes darkened two shades as he came toward me and that was something I'd swear on no matter what.

"The nudity?" he asked quietly. I didn't have to answer. "I promise you, Modestie, that you'll be beautiful on the screen. Actually..." He stepped back to appraise me. "I can't think of another woman men would want to see naked more right now. You're every man's fantasy. The badass Araya of Gassar."

"That's a character." My throat was suddenly dry. "And I don't care what every man wants to see. I'm not doing it." I moved to go around him, but he blocked my path and I was about to make a very bad decision.

Making a scene would land me on every gossip

or news site on the internet. It would make my personal life the story and that wasn't what I wanted. In that moment, I resolved to not allow Anison Brecht to determine my narrative.

I'd hold my own but would tread lightly. He was one of the most powerful men in Hollywood right now. Instead, I clutched my glass of water closer to my chest, suddenly regretting the decision to wear something with such a low-cut front. Nobody could see anything, but between that and the open back, I now felt naked. Thanks to the creepy guy leering at me right now.

Being so focused on Anison, I didn't notice someone else approach until an arm slid around my shoulders and a voice I hadn't heard in several years said, "Sorry I took so long, baby." Then he kissed the side of my head.

Scrambling for words, any words, a syllable would do, I slowly moved my gaze from Anison to the man standing beside me.

Thatcher Hoffman. Tall with tidy, brown hair and the deepest dark eyes that for some reason always reminded me of chocolate. He stood beside me in a deep-blue suit looking every bit the sexy man that I'd seen on the internet for the last three years.

"I-It's OK." Those words were hard to push out.

Then Thatcher turned to Anison and said, "I'm Thatcher Hoffman."

"Bass player for Forever 18," I added.

Anison introduced himself, but neither man reached out to shake the other's hand. Instead, they stood in a stare down. Anison's jaw was tight in what looked like barely controlled anger while Thatcher acted like he didn't have a care in the world. He had his arm around me still, his hand giving my shoulder a reassuring squeeze, but the rest of him was totally relaxed.

He tossed back the last of his drink then set the glass on the nearest surface. I think it was a table, but I couldn't keep my eyes off him, so I never looked.

It had been almost five years since I'd seen him in person.

When I'd left Michigan, Thatcher and I had stayed in touch, but it had been calls and texts. Even those had tapered off after a while with both of us so busy that it was hard to keep up.

"You finished with that?" He pointed at my glass. I took one more sip to ease the dryness in my throat then handed him the glass, which he, I assumed, set with his own. "I'm going to steal my girl for a few minutes." He directed that at Anison, but his eyes stayed firmly on mine.

I bit into my bottom lip to hide the relief washing through me.

Getting me away from that man was the only thing I wanted. And this was the perfect excuse.

Thatcher took my hand in his then led me through a group of people until he could pull me through a French door out onto a secluded patio. This might have been where people went to smoke, but there was no one out here and we were on the opposite side of the parking lot.

It was quiet and private.

"You OK?" he asked.

The only thing I could think to do was throw myself into his arms and squeeze as tightly as I could. I might not have been super strong, but he'd at least feel it.

He wrapped his arms around me, his hands sliding over my bare back, then dropped his chin to the top of my head.

"Is that a *yes*?" he asked quietly.

After I pulled away enough to look up at him, but not so far as for him not to still have his hands on me, I answered, "I am now." A little bit of my French accent came out with those words. It happened. "How did you know I needed rescuing?"

He snorted. "Just everything. The look on your

face. Your body language. The way you were gripping that fucking glass like you might shatter it at any second."

"Thank you," I told him quietly.

"Who was that?"

I furrowed my brows before remembering that Thatcher was in the music world and not the movie one. Most people would know who Anison was when hearing his name but might not have known what he looked like.

"Anison Brecht."

He cocked his head to the side. "The director?" I nodded quickly, my hair brushing against my back and his hand, which was still scorching my skin. "Why the fuck did you look so uncomfortable?"

I blew out a hard breath. "Now that's a bit of a story."

Thatcher swallowed hard. "Lovers' quarrel?"

I pulled my lips back across my teeth in disgust. "He wishes, but no."

Now his muscles hardened and his jaw clenched. "I'm going to need that story before I go in and break his neck."

"Please don't do that." I walked over to the ledge on the little half-wall that surrounded the patio and sat, allowing the flowy skirt of my dress to float down to my feet, hoping that he'd do the same.

It took a few seconds, but he followed. "I don't like how that sounded," he admitted.

I smiled. "Can I ask how you're doing first?"

He snorted. "Yeah. I'm good. The last three years have been insane."

"I know. I've seen some things online."

He wet his bottom lip and ran a hand down the back of my head. "I should've called."

I shrugged. "We both probably should have, but we both have insane lives. Though I've just come off a little sabbatical and I highly recommend it."

"Yeah." He chuckled. "I'll see if I can get my manager to pencil that in."

He considered me for a moment before asking his next question. Sitting beside Thatcher again had me swirling with emotions. He was beautiful and had grown so much into a man since the last time I'd seen him. His arms filled out his suit and he looked every bit the part of a *GQ* model. But something told me that there were things I wasn't seeing.

Thatcher had never been the clean-cut, preppy kind of guy, though his hair was usually as short as it was now. Very short on the side with the longer faux-hawk top. He hadn't had that in high school, but he'd still always kept it short. Or at least for the year that I'd been at their school.

"Am I going to be fucking something up for you?" he asked.

"What do you mean?"

"I mean..." He pointed to indicate inside and what had just happened. "A hundred people, if they were watching, saw me slide in and kiss the side of your head. They heard me call you 'baby' and drag you away from that guy. Is there a boyfriend who we're going to have to explain things to? Because I will. I don't want to fuck anything up for you."

Oh. Right. A boyfriend. "No. There's no boyfriend to explain anything to. And I don't think anyone was watching."

"What about the director?"

I shrugged. "I'm thinking he won't say anything because he wouldn't want anything said about him."

Thatcher scratched at the back of his head. "I need you to explain that. You were so fucking uncomfortable with that guy. What gives?"

I took a deep breath then blew it out slowly. "That director is the biggest in Hollywood right now and he has a movie he wants me to do. I'm trying to cross over from the teen star of a huge franchise to an adult actress and he thinks he's the way for me to do it."

"'Adult' actress?" Humor made the corners of his mouth twitch. "I'll be honest, I never pictured you doing porn, but I'm here to tell you I'll pay to see it and will be your biggest fan."

I slapped a hand over my face as my skin flushed. "I didn't mean that kind of adult actress and you know it."

He gently pulled my hand away as his laughter shook not only him, but me, too. "I know. I'm just fucking with you. Why don't you want to do the movie? Is the script bad?"

That was when I remembered that Thatcher and I had spent quite a bit of time discussing my career when I'd been in Michigan. I'd known then that as soon as I could, I'd take the reins of my career into my own hands.

"I don't know," I told him truthfully. "I haven't read it. I'd guess it's not bad at all, given that he's the highest-grossing director right now."

"Then why don't you want to do it? Sounds like what you're looking for, right? My guess is it's something to do with *him* and my imagination is running fucking wild right now."

"It could be." I ran my hands down the front of

my dress in what was, probably, an unattractive move. "But I don't want to work with him and there are requirements that I'm not willing to meet."

"Like?" he prodded.

"First of all, the nudity," I explained. His jaw tightened. "I don't know that I want to be naked on screen ever, but I certainly don't want to do it now."

"Then you shouldn't. Was that fucker trying to pressure you into doing it? What'd he say?"

I had to smile at how it seemed that no time had passed between Thatcher and me. Between him and the other guys in the band, I'd felt rather well-protected in Saginaw that year. Anytime someone had been bothering me about being the chosen one, or when one of the other boys at school had wanted to be able to say they'd fucked an actress, Thatcher or one of his friends had stepped in and I'd known I'd been safe.

It was a lot like right now.

I'd also spent a lot of time in the garage listening to them play. They were good and I knew that after some hard work perfecting their sound that good things would happen for them.

"He said that I'm every man's fantasy and they all want to see me naked."

"Well, that's probably true."

My mouth dropped open and I didn't give it a thought before I slapped his arm. *"Thatcher!"*

His laughter made it hard to be mad at him. "What? It is. You're beautiful, Modestie. You've always been beautiful."

I sighed. "Thank you, but I want to be taken seriously and I don't care what every man's fantasy is. I don't want to do the movie."

"Is that the only reason he makes you uncomfortable?"

I bit my lips together without meaning to because it was the easiest way to give away that I had more to say.

"Tell me."

I swallowed hard and looked him in the eye. It was hard to do, but I hadn't done anything wrong and had nothing to be ashamed of. And this was *Thatcher*.

"After I left Michigan, I went back to filming Gassar. But a movie came up that my dad and Brian thought would make a great steppingstone for my post-Araya life. It wasn't a starring role, but I'd have a bit of screen time and be able to stretch my acting muscles."

"I've seen that series many times, Modestie. You stretch your acting muscles all over the place."

Giving him a small grin, I told him, "Thank you. But this was supposed to be more mainstream."

"And?

I sighed again. "Anison was the director and..." I rolled my eyes because it shouldn't have been this difficult to explain to Thatcher. He was my safe space. "Anison made it clear that he wanted to give me the part, but that I'd also have to do something for him." Thatcher tensed but waited for me to continued, only now I couldn't look him in the eye. "He said that he and I would have a lot of fun on set and he'd teach me everything I needed to know about a man."

Rage took over Thatcher's beautiful features before he said in a voice too calm for his words, "I'm going to go kill that motherfucker."

5

THATCHER

That director was lucky he was still alive.

I'd never killed a man before, but right now, I had enough rage in me to do it. It'd get ugly. I'd go to prison. The band would have to replace me, but it would've been worth never seeing that look on Modestie's face again.

"You're not going to kill him," she told me as we sat outside the hotel where the premiere afterparty was being held. Her amber eyes sparkled in the light and I'd forgotten just how lost I could get in them.

How lost I had gotten in them once.

"I think I am."

She shook her head back and forth, though a smile played on her lips. "There's no reason for murder."

I ran a hand down the silky, exposed skin of her back. "How old were you?"

She wet her lips quickly and looked away. "Seventeen. I didn't turn eighteen until a couple of weeks later.

Now, I was even more pissed off. She was a fucking minor. "He said he'd give you a part if you fucked him, Modestie. Seems like a good enough reason to me to kill him. Add in that you were a minor and he'll be lucky to die quickly."

"That was years ago and I'm a big girl. I can handle myself."

"Like in there?" I snapped, instantly regretting the fact that I was saying she couldn't handle herself. "You looked like you were trying to melt into the wall."

She furrowed her brows. "He had me backed into a corner. I was handling it." She wet her lips again. "But I can't say that I don't appreciate you stepping in. I did have it handled, but with him, it quickly could've become something else."

"So he offers you a part if you fuck him, is now desperate to get you naked on screen, and he makes you feel unsafe at a party?" I shook my head. "Sounds like a good reason to kill him."

She giggled. Every time I spoke, I added a reason to justify what I wanted to do to him.

"Would you stop with all the killing talk? I haven't seen you in five years. I'd rather talk about what you've been doing. Do you have a girlfriend who might also be worried if our little performance in there hits the tabloids? Kids? I assume rock stars have kids they don't know about."

Now it was my turn to laugh. "No girlfriend, and no kids that I know of."

It looked like she wanted to say something else, but instead, we sat there silently until she finally stood. "I should be going. My PA, Margot, was supposed to be here tonight but she tripped and fell so she had to go get an Xray. I want to check on her. And I'm sure I'm in for at least a dozen angry calls in the morning."

"From?" I pushed to my feet, too.

"My agent, Brian. My father. Take your pick. They'll be upset about that run-in with Anison."

"Fuck them."

Modestie let out a loud laugh, like there was an inside joke that I didn't know. She didn't let me in on what was so funny.

"I'll walk you out," I told her.

After getting to the front of the hotel, we were

waiting for her car when I asked, "Do you have your phone on you?"

Her eyebrows shot up in surprise. "Always." She reached into a hidden pocket on her dress and pulled it out. Hidden to me anyway because that dress didn't look like it had pockets, but I knew very well how excited women got when a dress they loved had them.

"Let me put my number in. It's not the same one from when I was in high school." I held the phone up closer to her face to unlock it then went to her contacts to put my number in. Once I was done, I told her, "Use it whenever you want to. If you need to talk or whatever. We're in town for a few days but even after that. Now that I've seen you again, I don't want to lose touch again."

"Thank you." Her full lips curved into a smile before she climbed into the car that came to a stop in front of her.

The last thing I wanted to do was watch her drive away.

But I did it anyway.

THE NEXT MORNING, I woke to my phone ringing incessantly.

Who would call me so fucking early?

My house was quiet since I lived alone and although the guys and I had hired a service to maintain our places while we were on the road, even they'd know not to come so fucking early if I was home.

I touched the area on my phone screen where I thought the answer button would be then raised it to my ear without checking the caller ID or opening my eyes. "What?"

"I woke you," the sweetest voice I'd ever heard said quietly into the phone, causing me to spring upright in my bed.

"What's wrong?" I assumed there had to be something if she was calling me at... I pulled the phone away to check the time. *Shit.* Ten-thirty. It wasn't that early, but I hadn't gone to bed until around five.

"I'm sorry I woke you." A bit more of her French accent came through than normally did. She'd told me when we'd been in school that her father had insisted she be raised bilingual from the start, so she'd had an English tutor and had been successful at getting rid of almost all traces of her accent. He wanted it to make her more adaptable for movies.

"I don't care about that. What's going on?" I

threw the covers off me and hopped out of bed. I had a feeling that whatever was going on, I'd need pants for it.

She sighed, her breath feathering over the phone. "Are you hungry? Can we get breakfast?"

Clearly, whatever it was, she wanted to talk about it in person. "Yeah. Of course."

"Do you want to meet somewhere? Or I could grab food and come to your place."

"Come here," I told her immediately. That way, I could shower really quickly before she arrived, figuring it'd take her at least twenty minutes to half an hour at best. "I'll text you my address."

Modestie didn't ask what I'd want for breakfast and honestly, I didn't care. Whatever she brought, I'd eat.

After sending her my address, I hurried to the bathroom to get cleaned up with all kinds of crazy things running through my head as to why she might've been coming over this morning. Most of them weren't good. Though a couple of them I could've really gotten behind and so I let my imagination run a bit wild, which woke my cock right up.

If I would've had time to rub one out right then and there, I would've and it would've been to thoughts of Modestie. But the last thing I wanted to do was be caught with my dick in my hand while she was outside ringing my doorbell.

It ended up taking her forty minutes. By the time she'd arrived, I'd showered; skipped shaving and left my hair messy; brushed my teeth; and pulled on a pair of jeans; a dark blue T-shirt; and black Vans.

Took longer than I thought because I'd just finished up when my doorbell rang.

When I pulled the door open, Modestie stood before me with her golden hair down in waves over her shoulders and large, round dark sunglasses over her eyes, making her look every bit the part of movie star. She was wearing a summer kind of dress that had a deep V between her breasts, though not as deep as that little number she'd worn last night. There was a large band around her waist, making it look even smaller than I knew it was, which flared out into a skirt that fell just above her knees. And she was wearing flat, barely there, sandals.

As I opened the door wider, Modestie came close enough that I could take the bag from her as well as the drink carrier.

"There's a French bakery not far from where my assistant, Margot, is looking for a house for me. It also happens to not be so far from here," she explained. "I brought a few croissants, *pain au chocolat*, a baguette, and jams. I wasn't sure what you'd want, but all of that sounded good to me. And for the drinks I got a café au lait, and a regular black coffee because I don't know how you take your coffee. The other two containers are orange juice."

I furrowed my brows. "How many people did you think are eating with us this morning?"

She shrugged, gesturing around her. "I wanted you to have options and how would I know if you had someone here with you?"

With Modestie following behind me, I headed to the kitchen, where I set the goodies on the small table where I ate most of my meals when I was home. Scratch that. Most were eaten in the living room in front of the TV, at least when I was alone or it was just us guys. Then I turned to her.

"You think I invited you over here while I was with another woman?"

Her fingers tangled with the sunglasses she now had in her hands. "I don't know what you do, Thatcher."

I took a step closer. "Not that." Then I paused a moment to see her reaction before pointing at one of the seats. "You can sit. I'll grab plates."

Once I had everything we needed, I settled down in the chair nearest the one she'd taken. She began pulling all the containers out of the bag and setting things up. It wasn't until she was satisfied that I broached the subject.

Damn. This croissant was melting in my mouth. "So, what gives? What happened?"

She put a small pieces of pastry in her mouth. "Well, since I woke you up, I know you haven't seen anything. You would've said something as soon as you got to the door." She looked up at me. "I think." Modestie reached into the pocket on her dress and pulled out her phone. I was beginning to think everything she wore had pockets.

Then she held it up to me.

Another Member of Forever 18 Finds Love.

That was the headline on some gossip site that I didn't recognize the name of. OK. It wasn't a secret that some of the guys had fallen hard for their girlfriends. But then I scrolled down and there was a picture of Modestie and me from the patio last night. One where she was in my arms and my head was resting on top of hers.

My eyes were closed and even I had to admit that I looked fucking happy to have her there.

Because I had been.

Fuck I wish I had a copy of that picture.

"OK?" Because I didn't understand the problem.

People said shit about actresses and musicians all the time. I didn't give a fuck.

"I had some very angry calls from my agent this morning. That I should've cleared it with him or at least let him know that I was going public with my *relationship*." The way she enunciated the word told me all I needed to know about how her agent felt about the rumor. "He went on about the *image* I'm supposed to maintain. Of the good girl who I needed to at least appear to be."

I sat back and ran my hand over my bottom lip, trying not to let her see how funny I thought that was. Not her being a good girl, whatever the fuck that meant. But how being with me would ruin that.

"I take it he doesn't think I fit the image," I said once I knew I wouldn't be laughing.

She shrugged while letting her eyes roam up my body, taking in the tattoos she could see. "I guess not. I basically told him to fuck off. That the picture was just a timing thing and that we were friends in high school."

"What'd he say?"

She sighed deeply then took a drink of the orange juice. "He said, 'A rock star, Modesty? Really? You know how they are. You're going to be everywhere when he's seen with someone else and you're the girl next door. The girl next door isn't meant to be with the bad boy. This isn't a fucking romance novel.'"

I chuckled. "He sounds like a dick."

"He is."

"Why are you still with him, then?"

She waved me off. "Different conversation for a different time."

"And why the fuck does he say your name like that? 'Modesty'?"

This time, she rolled her eyes. "He's the only person I actually know... who's actually *met* me who has an issue pronouncing my name."

"That's fucking disrespectful." My phone buzzed several times as it lay on the table, but I ignored it. This was more important. Whatever was happening on my phone could wait. She had all my attention.

"I can't disagree with you there, but again... Conversation for a different time."

"OK." But I'd hold her to that. "So, does this bother you? That there's a rumor out there about us, apparently?'"

"No." She ran her tongue over her bottom lip. "I don't care about rumors and I really don't care if people think we're together. Hell, it'd probably help keep assholes like Anison Brecht away from me, but I was worried it's going to cause you problems."

"Me?" That wasn't something I could understand. "How the fuck would it be a problem for me if the gossip sites link me to a huge star who's beautiful and sexy?" I brushed my hand through my hair. "Nah. I think that could only help me."

Modestie bit her lips together, but the smile still came through. "I meant with the band. If my agent's freaking out about it, I was worried your manager would be too. Or that it would cause problems for your... lifestyle."

Other women. That was what she was worried about?

"I don't have that kind of relationship with my manager, baby. He doesn't care where I put my dick as long as I show up to soundcheck and for the show."

She flinched at my wording but didn't say anything about it. "Your phone's going off a lot. How do you know he's not upset?"

While smirking, I grabbed my phone and opened my texts then turned it to her so she could see that not one of them was from Sean. There were many from Jamison, it seemed, and some from the other guys asking if it was all true.

"See?"

"OK." She sat back in the chair like a weight had been lifted. "I'm sure it'll die down anyway. It's two pictures."

"Listen." I reached out, grabbed the chair she was sitting in and pulled it until she was between my legs. "If your agent is that fucking controlling and gets angry over your personal life, you really should consider getting a new one."

"I know," she agreed. "I'm working on it, but he is one of the best agents out there. He's been mine for so long, chosen by my father, that I'm not sure I even know how to choose another one."

"I bet Sean could help with that. He knows fucking everyone."

She nodded gently. "Margot would probably kiss you if you helped me get a new agent. She hates Brian."

"Margot doesn't like him?"

"She hates him with a passion and wants me to tell him to kick rocks. Her words. I assume it's an American expression."

I laughed loudly because I couldn't help it. "It is. But Margot's not the one I'd want to kiss me anyway. But it sounds like I'd like her."

"You would, I'm sure. Everyone does." Her eyes

met mine. "Except Brian," we both said at the same time, causing us both to laugh.

We went back to our breakfast, but I didn't move her chair back and neither did she. It was only a few more bites before the best idea I'd ever had came to mind.

"Why don't we just let people think it's true?"

"Think what's true?" She took another drink of juice.

"That we're together."

She sputtered on the liquid, causing it to spray up into her face, but only onto her upper lip.

"What?" She reached blindly for a napkin.

"Yeah. It pisses your agent off, you said. Which is a good thing. It might keep that asshole from last night at bay at least for a little while. It's a win-win."

"Um..." She dabbed her napkin over her mouth to make sure she'd gotten all the juice. "That only sounds like a win for me."

I shook my head. "Nah. Knowing that the horny bastard from last night is off your scent is a win for me, too. Plus, like I said, there's no downside for me if people think we're together."

Her face softened and she placed her hand gently on mine. "I appreciate the offer, but I can't ask you to do that, Thatcher."

"You didn't ask. It's my idea."

Our gazes connected and this heat rose between us. It was so present that I thought I could reach out and touch it. Maybe pretending to be together would be hard, considering I'd have to touch her sometimes without actually being able to *touch* her. But no one would believe that we were together yet never make contact.

"I think that sounds fantastic," she finally said. "As long as you're sure."

"I am."

If I couldn't have Modestie Dubois for real, pretending was the next best thing.

Even if it was the hardest thing I'd ever have to do.

6

MODESTIE

I'd shown up at Thatcher's house two days ago to apologize for the trouble coming his way after those photographs had hit the internet and I'd left with a fake boyfriend who didn't seem to be getting anything out of the arrangement.

In reality, I shouldn't have needed a fake boyfriend whom everyone knew to keep the creepy-ass director out of my personal space. I was an adult. *No* should've been enough. But there was only so far I could push Anison Brecht without getting black-balled by my entire industry.

He had the power. I had some power, given the success of the Gassar series, but he had more. He wasn't just the biggest director whose movies all made more money than anything should ever make.

He was in tight with studio heads, and the fear of being run out of the industry loomed heavily over a lot of actors' heads.

This meant that if things went too badly with Anison Brecht, other actors could refuse to work with me to reduce the guilt by association. I couldn't be the black sheep when I was just trying to get my groove back.

The me too movement had helped show a lot of these problems but even a single comment could land me in court with no guarantee of winning. It was my word against his.

"You know you already have enough money to never work again, right?" Margot asked as I got ready to meet Thatcher.

I'd insisted that he and I get together to go over the parameters of this fake relationship. Kind of like meeting with an intimacy coordinator. We both needed to know the other's boundaries. He didn't know that was why we were meeting yet.

"That's not the point and you know it," I told her back. It wasn't about money. Acting was something that I loved doing.

"You know Brian didn't send the scripts over that you asked for."

It wasn't a question, but my eyes locked with hers in the mirror and she raised a brow.

The man was testing my patience.

"I know. I gave him a couple of days, so I'm going to stop over there after I meet up with Thatcher."

"You'd think that you'd make meeting your boyfriend sound better than a business meeting."

It took everything in me to not look at her this time. She'd see through it all. Not even Margot could know this was fake, even though I trusted the woman with my life. She'd never tell my secrets to anyone, but I couldn't chance someone overhearing the two of us talking. Not if this was to be believable.

"I'm just in a hurry."

"Mm-hmm." She looked down at her iPad, which told me she was moving on. "You have the charity event tomorrow night. Your dress will be delivered today. I'll be here waiting on that. I did find a few places that you should look at. Let me know when you have the chance and I'll set that up for you." Now she glanced up at me. "Are you planning on staying here until we find somewhere for you?"

"Yes. I like it here." And it helped that this suite of rooms was large enough to be an apartment on its own.

"OK, I'll make sure the hotel is aware."

That was my Margot. Making sure everything I needed got taken care of.

"All right." I pushed up from the vanity, where I'd been doing my makeup. "I'm going to go. I'll be back in time for my appointment with Harriet, though I don't know why I need a dry run on hair and makeup."

"So that you look perfect?"

I snapped my fingers as if I'd forgotten. "Oh. Right."

After a quick goodbye, I hurried out of the suite and the hotel. Margot had a car waiting for me so that I wouldn't have to worry about maneuvering through L.A. myself. A lot of the time, she drove me herself or I walked. Once I got settled, I'd buy a car, but that was low on the list right now.

Thatcher had offered to pick me up, but since I had to go to Brian's office after, I'd declined. Instead, I showed up back at his house empty-handed, which felt weird, but he'd insisted he'd get lunch for us. I wasn't very hungry and didn't care about the food, but it gave me something to do with my hands so I wasn't just sitting there staring at Thatcher.

"Hey," he answered as he pulled the door open. "You look great."

I'd just put on a dress similar to the one I'd worn

when I'd come over the other day. My hair was down with soft curls and I'd done a natural makeup. There was no need for me to glam up just to go to his house.

"Thank you." I stepped through the door so he could close it behind me.

"I thought we could eat at the coffee table in the living room. The kitchen table seems too formal. This will be more comfortable."

"I like comfort."

I followed him into his living room and got my first look around.

Thatcher didn't live in some huge mansion in the hills. His house was basically a bungalow. A large bungalow, but still a bungalow on the beach. I didn't know how many bedrooms there were, but I'd guess three. All of it was very homey and had a comfortable, lived-in feel to it.

"I didn't want something bigger," he told me.

"What?"

"The house." He waved his arms around. "I didn't want something bigger because I'm not here very much of the year. Seemed like a waste."

Oh. He was talking about the house. "I can understand that. My flat in Paris is large, but not what a lot of people would picture me living in."

He sat on one side of the couch then turned,

tucking one leg under the other so he'd be facing where I sat. So I toed off my shoes and did the same thing. Might as well get comfortable.

"What about here?" he asked. "Where do you live?"

"A hotel. Margot is looking for a place for me, but for now, the hotel."

The two of us made ourselves a plate from the Chinese food spread that he had laid out on the table. After putting a little bit of everything on my plate, I grabbed a pair of chopsticks and sat back.

"I wasn't sure what you like," he told me. "Hell, I wasn't even sure if you like Chinese food, so I have some backups in the fridge."

Him being so considerate brought a smile to my face. "Not liking Chinese food is un-American, isn't it?"

"You're not American," he countered and I couldn't argue with him there.

"True. But I'm not a picky eater." I hadn't been allowed to be when I'd been a kid and it was one of the few things that I could be grateful to my father about. He didn't control how much I ate as long as I was eating healthily and not gaining a pound more than necessary for my growth. "I'll put just about anything in my mouth."

Thatcher sputtered, like he was choking on the piece of chicken he'd just put in his mouth. Then he coughed twice and reached for his drink. Once he got settled down, he said, "Fuck, Modestie. You can't say shit like that when I'm eating."

Stifling my giggle, I asked, "Is that one of the rules?"

He raised an eyebrow. "Rules?"

"Yeah. If we're doing this fake relationship thing, don't we need rules? Like what's allowed."

"Well, we shouldn't tell anyone." He took another bite.

"Of course. If anyone besides the two of us knew we were faking this, it'd be a disaster. Not for you, though. You're a rock star. Any behavior is accepted. But it'd make me look like I'm too sensitive to handle a grabby director. Like I'll be a problem on the set or something."

His jaw tightened. "You shouldn't have to *handle* a grabby director."

"I know. And outside of Anison Brecht, everyone I've worked with has been totally respect-ful. Even the love scenes I had to do in the Gassar series. My costar, Evan, was as careful as could be. The director was patient with both of us because we were young. Because of all that patience, I think we put out something great. It even seemed natural." I'd been eighteen, but still so young in so many ways.

"*I* knew you were faking." His voice was lower, causing my skin to heat up.

"Yeah, well, *you* would."

He chuckled before taking another bite. "I have to be able to touch you."

Now it was my turn to choke on my food. "What?" It took three more coughs to clear it up.

"If you're mine, people will expect me to touch you. It'd be weird if I didn't."

"Oh, right." That made sense. "I trust you, Thatcher. I don't have a problem with you touching me."

His gaze burned into mine and while we both knew we were talking about the innocent touches of a couple in public, there was something else brimming underneath.

This was going to be hard. Thatcher had been the one man in my life who genuinely cared about me, about my thoughts and feelings. Falling in love with him seemed like a given. But we were friends and I'd just gotten him back in my life. I couldn't chance losing him again.

"You have to come on tour with us the day after

tomorrow." He broke the silence that was steaming up the room.

"What?" I didn't think I'd heard him correctly.

"You have to come on tour. At least for a little while. Visits and shit. Whatever fits your schedule." He set his plate on the table while I continued to hold mine, even though I was already full. "Nobody is going to believe that we just got together and I left you behind. Not to mention, I don't like the idea of you on your own with that asshole still pressuring you." Our eyes locked again. "Plus, I feel like you could use a break."

"I just had a long break," I countered.

"Yeah."

But again, so many unsaid things hung between us. I knew what my unsaid things were, but I desperately wished I knew his.

"Well, right now, I'm just going to be reading through some scripts. I can do that on a tour bus," I told him. "Won't I be in the way?"

He shook his head. "I'm going to talk to the guys tonight. We already thought we needed a second bus now. With the guys bringing their girls. Not to mention Jamison fucking hates it that Avalon spends her nights in Lennox's bunk." He glanced up at me. "That's his sister."

"Ouch."

"Yeah, exactly. So we'll get another bus and some will move over. It'll be fine." He leaned across the couch so that his face was close enough to mine to kiss. My heart sputtered against my chest. "You'll have to sleep in my bunk with me."

My mouth was suddenly as dry as the acridest desert in the world. Sleep. With Thatcher. And not in a fun way, but just sleep all night right next to him.

It made sense but was something I hadn't thought about.

"Right. Yeah. Of course."

To keep from allowing the hyena laughter that was threatening to bubble up from doing so, I leaned forward, forcing Thatcher to sit back so that I could set my plate on the table and look at my phone for the time.

"I have to go," I told him. More time had passed than I'd realized.

"Now?"

"Yeah." I pushed forward and slid my shoes on. Did I have to leave right this minute? No. I had time before my appointment with Harriet that I could've stayed a while longer and still stopped by Brian's office. But if I stayed here with him one second longer, I worried that I'd attack him. In a sexy way.

It'd been a long time since I'd had sex. It'd been a long time since there'd been someone I'd *wanted* to have sex with. But Thatcher was making it very close to me attacking him and ruining everything.

"I have to go by Brian's office," I told him. He made a sound in the back of his throat that told me he didn't approve. "I have to pack something to go on tour, right? Then I have to meet with my hair and makeup team to do a test run for tomorrow night."

"The charity event?"

"Yes." I pushed to my feet and then turned to him slowly. "Would you... want to go with me?" I hadn't taken a date to an event ever and wasn't sure this was the time to do it, but if we were going to put this out there, then we might as well go full balls out.

I twisted my fingers together. I'd never in my life asked a guy to go out with me and it didn't matter if this was a real date or not. It was Thatcher, so I shouldn't even have been nervous, yet the way my stomach was clenching, I knew I was.

The corners of his mouth turned upward, not quite a smile, but something more than nothing. "Of course. Can you text me the details? I'll get Lilah to put an outfit together."

I swallowed hard. "Lilah?"

He tapped my nose with his index finger. "Our stylist."

My shoulders released the tension they'd been holding. The last thing I wanted to do was come between him and whatever he had going on in his life. And Thatcher was a good guy, which meant that he'd try to take care of me no matter what. Another woman might not have understood that.

But I had to trust him. He said there wasn't anyone in his life.

He was suddenly standing in front of me. "She's with Grayson," he explained, though I hadn't asked. "Modestie, I wouldn't screw someone over. If I had someone in my life, even casually, I'd tell you."

"Right. Yeah. I know."

Yet all of this was moving so fast that I worried I'd get swept up in it. So I'd have to constantly remind myself that anything Thatcher did that was beyond the friendship that we'd always had was fake. He was pretending. Acting. I was very accustomed to that.

He walked me out of his house and to the car I'd called back then told me goodbye. There were no goodbye kisses because why would there have been? We weren't in front of an audience yet.

Then I was off to Brian's office.

As I walked through the lobby, Brian's assistant, Hilary, a young, beautiful dark haired girl who'd been working for him for two years, was there looking down at her phone. I didn't have an appointment, so I knew she wasn't waiting for me. Though I wondered why she was down here and not in the office.

"Hey, Hilary," I told her as I passed, but I came to a stop when her head snapped up.

"Hi, Modestie." Her brows furrowed. "Do you have an appointment today?" Her finger tapped against her phone frantically, like she'd forgotten I was coming.

"I don't." I reached out and set my hand on hers so she'd stop freaking out. "I'm just here because Brian didn't send the scripts that I asked for."

She shook her head. "He's such an asshole."

That, I couldn't disagree with and I had to choke back a laugh. She probably didn't mean to say that to me. "What're you doing down here?"

"Waiting for—"

Another woman slid in beside us like she'd just entered behind me. She had short, brown hair and these beautiful brown eyes. She was about Hilary's height, which was a lot taller than me. When she looked at me, her eyes grew wide.

"Oh my god," she said with excitement.

"Modestie," Hilary began. "This is my friend Vanessa. Obviously, a big fan."

"It's so nice to meet you." Vanessa shook my hand fervently.

"Nice to meet you, too." I tried holding back a laugh.

"We're going to lunch," Hilary told me while pushing her friend away. "Brian's up there. I'll see you later."

With a smile, I headed to the elevator.

Without Hilary there, I'd just have to talk to the secretary. The older woman with the severe face and tight bun who thought she was protecting Brian from a gang of assassins rather than his clients.

Shockingly, she insisted Brian wasn't in. He was handling some client business. Yeah. Right. He was probably right behind the door of his office but knew why I was there.

Still, the secretary, whose name I couldn't remember because Brian went through secretaries like most people went through underwear, called him. I listened hard to see if I could hear his voice in the office, but his walls were thick.

Once she was done, she smiled sweetly at me. "He told me where the scripts are. I'll be right back."

True to her word, she was back with three thick envelopes that looked brand new. As in, it didn't look like Brian had them prepared to send. My guess was, he hadn't planned to send them at all and had hoped I'd forget about it.

Shaking my head, I took them from her then left the hellscape that was his office.

The longer this went on, the more I was sure that Brian's and my time together was quickly coming to an end.

I'd have to deal with my father when I actually pulled the plug, but it'd be worth it.

For now, I was going to focus on Thatcher and the fact that I was going on tour with one of the hottest bands in the world.

7

THATCHER

"I fucking hate you," Lilah said as she threw her hands in the air and Grayson snickered from his seat on his couch.

"What?" I looked up at her with eyes as innocent as I could muster. I knew exactly why she hated me right now.

Lilah's chocolate hair was pulled back into a bun and she was standing before us in long, khaki shorts and a pink tank top. She had a clothing bag hanging over her one arm and another bag in her other.

"You know exactly why I hate you right now." She stomped out of the living room into one of Grayson's spare rooms, cursing under her breath as if we couldn't still hear her. Then she was back with her hands on her hips.

"Gray," I said to him, but I didn't take my eyes off her. "You need to handle your woman."

He groaned. "Why do you want to cause yourself problems?"

I snickered at the entire situation. "Look." I stood to my full height, which was a lot more than Lilah had to offer, but she wasn't intimidated by any of us. Nor did I want her to be. "You didn't have to go shopping for me. I just asked your opinion. That's all. I said I'd find something in my closet."

She made a disgusted sound that stayed in the back of her throat as she rolled her eyes. Lilah pushed past me in the kitchen then reappeared with a bottle of water.

"Of course I had to shop for you," she finally said after draining a bit of the water. "It's my job."

"But this isn't a band thing."

"True. But people know I'm your stylist and if you show up to the Carlisle Gala in a fucking T-shirt and jeans, it'll ruin whatever reputation I've gained by making sure the band doesn't look like a barbershop quartet or a bunch of teenagers who never had a mother."

Grayson chuckled behind me. "We can dress ourselves, baby."

Her entire face pinched together like she'd smelled something awful. "Barely."

Lilah was mad. That was the only explanation as to why she was saying those things. We dressed ourselves fine. Now, granted, it wasn't for anything like this. The Carlisle Gala was an exclusive charity event. Only certain people were invited and they were all recognizable names. It was probably one of the fancier events in L.A. You had to be invited and if you accepted, your donation was mighty. It all went to some kind of animal conservation effort or something.

I'd have to ask Modestie for more details.

I was incredibly curious how much this night was costing Modestie. And if she'd originally planned to go alone, I wondered how adding me worked. The band made a bunch of money now but it wasn't Modestie kind of money.

"It's the Carlisle Gala, Thatcher. A little warning would've been nice."

I threw my hands in the air. "Listen, you knew almost as soon as I did. She asked me yesterday."

Lilah let out a sigh. "I can't believe you're going with Modestie Dubois."

Grayson piped up. "We all knew her in high school."

"I know. But Modestie Dubois. She's a huge star."

Once again, I held my arms out in the air. "And what the fuck do you think we are?"

A smile played on Lilah's lips. She regularly forgot that we were kind of big as well. People stopped us in the streets for pictures and autographs. Women threw themselves at us, even though some of us had girlfriends.

But yeah. Modestie was a huge star.

"*Anyway,*" she stressed so I'd know to move on, "I had to go to six different stores to find the perfect suit for you. And with such short notice, you better not need any alterations."

She'd altered many things for us over the last months, but there was no way I'd expect her to do any of that today.

"I promise, no alterations. But suit? I thought we had to do tuxes for this."

She shook her head. "The Carlisle is black tie, but that means three-piece suit *or* tux. You don't strike me as a tux kind of guy. However, the three-piece suit is amazing and sexy."

"Hey, now." Grayson piped up from the couch. "We've been over this. Thatcher's not sexy. *I'm* sexy."

She rolled her eyes again. "Yeah. Yeah." Then she focused back on me. "Now go get naked."

Grayson groaned behind me, but I couldn't stop the laugh that bubbled out.

Lilah had seen all of us in various states of dress, given her job, but I thought Grayson was the only one she'd actually seen naked.

I hurried into the guest room and yanked my shirt over my head.

"Put everything on then come out or call me in," she said through the door. "I'll make sure it all fits the way it was supposed to."

A guy could get used to having someone pick out all of his clothes for him. I'd given Lilah Modestie's phone number so that she could text to find out whatever she needed to know about what Modestie is wearing. So we'd match or whatever.

It took me a few minutes to get into the damn thing with all the buttons on the dress shirt and all that shit. Luckily, my dad had taught me how to tie a tie. I even pulled the black dress shoes out because Lilah had said to put on everything.

Then I went out to the living room.

"Wow," she said when she saw me. "You look respectable."

"I can fool anyone."

She came over to me and did all of her checks, ran her hands over my shoulders, yanked on the jacket, then stepped back.

"I really outdid myself today." Yet she was still inspecting every part of me with her eyes.

The suit consisted of a dress shirt, dark blue vest, jacket and pants, and a dark blue and silver polka-dotted tie. She *had* outdone herself.

"Perfect," she said, stepping back. "Now take it off."

"Buy me dinner first," I said automatically.

She chuckled for a moment. "If you take it off now, I have time to get the shirt washed, dried, and ironed. I'll steam out the suit so there won't be a single wrinkle on it."

"You don't have to do all that," I told her. I was capable of washing a shirt.

"Do it. You reflect on me at these things. Are you picking Modestie up?"

I shook my head as a yanked at the tie on my way back to the bedroom. "She said she already hired a limo, so she'd pick me up."

Once I was changed, I sent Modestie a text saying she should pick me up here because Lilah wouldn't be done fussing until the last minute. Modestie didn't mind.

The gala started at seven. Modestie said she'd pick me up at six. With traffic and filing through the people, stopping for pictures on the carpet, we'd need at least that long.

Right at six, there was a knock on Grayson's door. All three of us headed to the entryway, even though I would've liked to greet her alone.

When I pulled open the door, Modestie took my damn breath away.

She was wearing a deep-blue dress that only had one strap over a single shoulder. That strap and the bodice were lined with silver sequins. There was a high-waisted belt that went around her and on the one side, more silver peeked out. Now I understood Lilah's color choices for me.

The dress was long, but not all one length. I was sure Lilah knew the exact word for it, but it was like layers of skirts, some short, some long, and she was wearing silver heels.

Fuck, she was beautiful.

Her golden hair was down, brushing her shoulders in curls.

"Are you going to let the woman in?" Grayson asked, snapping my attention away from her.

"Yeah. Sorry. Come in."

Modestie pursed her lips to keep her smile at bay. "You look great too," she whispered.

"This is Lilah," I told her.

Now her smile grew as she reached out her hand to shake Lilah's. "It's so nice to put a face to the person I've been texting all day."

"Well, these guys are terrible when it comes to fashion. And information. Or anything I might've needed to know for today."

"You did a fantastic job," she said after glancing at me again.

"Thank you. He almost looks respectable."

"Almost."

The two of them giggled and somehow, I knew right then that they were going to be friends. Lilah hadn't acted starstruck at meeting her and that said something. "Hey, Grayson." She reached over and gave him a friendly hug. "I haven't seen you in forever."

"Yeah, it's been a while, but you look beautiful."

"Thank you. But, uh, we should get going. Traffic."

I agreed and the two of us left Grayson and Lilah, like they were my parents wishing us a good night.

"You really do look beautiful," I told her once we were inside and the limo got moving.

"Thank you. It's easy to do when you have a team of people."

I nudged her knee. "Even without the team."

Her shy smile punched me in the heart. Which meant that I needed to change the topic.

"So," I began. "I've heard of the Carlisle Gala but don't really know what it's about. Also, how did you add me at the last minute?"

"It's a charity event for animal conservation. It was something my mother was passionate about. The animals. Not the gala. It didn't exist then. But she was passionate and I always knew that I wanted to make sure to step up in her place. I've gone or donated every year since I started making money. I haven't attended the last couple and thought it was time to get back to it."

"And adding me?"

"Oh, I didn't have to add you. Each year, I get an invitation for me and a plus one. I always buy the ticket for both, even though I go alone." She shrugged. "It all goes to try to save animals that might otherwise suffer and become extinct."

"You've never taken anyone else?"

She shook her head. "I've never had a fake boyfriend to take."

I didn't like the *fake* part of that statement because it was a reminder that this was all that she wanted. Modestie and I had always been clear on what we were and what we weren't.

And together for real was something we weren't.

"Your mom died, right?" I asked quietly.

She nodded and swallowed hard. "When I was still a baby." But she didn't elaborate on how and I wasn't about to ask.

We didn't have time for much more than that before we arrived at the venue. Then it was walking in, getting pictures, me obsessing about how fucking sexy Modestie looked, the way her body moved in that dress, and how her face lit up when she laughed at a comment I'd made.

I set my hand on her lower back as we took some photos together. Before long, these were the pictures everyone was going to be seeing rather than the ones from the other night. The gossip would still be there, but we were controlling the narrative now.

Modestie knew what to do and got us to our seats. Through dinner, we chatted with other sponsors of the charity. Surprisingly, the food was pretty good because usually the more formal the event the weirder the food got. While she spoke with some actors she apparently knew, I took a look at the silent auction items. That usually wasn't something I'd do, but when I saw one of them, I knew I needed to bid on it and make sure I won. So I filled out the information, including my credit card number so they could charge it when I won, then it was back to Modestie.

The only downside was that fucking director being there, but I'd given him a good enough stare down that he kept his distance from her. I wasn't even sure she knew he was there. That was how far he stayed from us.

By ten, we were ready to leave. The point of the whole thing was the donation.

Modestie's limo took us back to my house, but as I was getting out of the car, I asked, "Are you ready to go home?'

"No." Her answer was immediate and sure.

I reached out my hand so that she'd slide out then she told the driver that she'd text when she was ready to go home.

"Why don't I take you back to your hotel when you're ready?" I asked.

"I don't want to make you go out," she said. I gave her a pointed look. "OK." She leaned inside the car. "I'm done for the night. Thank you so much."

Then the limo drove away.

The two of us walked into my dark house, but sitting in my living room while we were dressed like this seemed ridiculous.

"Want to go for a walk on the beach?" I asked her. The nighttime walks on the beach were the best. The air was slightly cool, but the sand was still warm.

"Absolutely." She pushed her heels off and headed toward the patio door.

I did the same.

The two of us were walking on the sand right at the edge of the water with the moon shining down on us. It was a clear night and the waves gently lapping at the beach were relaxing. If we were really together, this would have been such a romantic setting to reach out, bring her face to mine... To just do anything.

"I never thought I'd be here with you again. Or anywhere," she told me quietly, which made my gut clench. I should've done a better job staying in touch.

"I'm sorry about that."

"Me too." She shivered with the next gust of wind, so I pulled my jacket off and draped it over the shoulders the way you always saw gentlemen do in the movies. I would've done it anyway, but that was what it reminded me of.

I undid the buttons on my vest as well as yanking off my tie. After shoving the tie in my pocket, I undid the cuff and rolled the sleeves a little.

This was better.

"Do you remember that night?" she asked, purposely not looking at me, I thought.

"Which?" Though I knew what she was talking about, I wanted to hear her say it.

She sighed quietly. "The night before I left."

"Remember it?" I chuckled. "I dreamed about it for at least a year."

She put her hands on my arm and pushed, though I didn't move much. "You did not."

"Uh, Modestie, I was a horny-all-the-fucking-time eighteen-year-old. Yeah, I fucking did."

Though I didn't think she knew I was watching her, she swallowed hard. "I thought only girls did that."

"Think about someone they've had sex with? No. That's pretty standard."

She twisted her fingers together in front of her and I didn't think she knew she was doing it. I was watching her but she was looking out in front of us.

"I meant that I was under the impression that I thought about it so much because it was my first time."

It had been her first time and I'd known that at the time. Even then, her wanting that with me had meant something. It had shown a trust that we'd built over the course of a year, even though I'd been the asshole to be having sex with other girls at that time. Though to be fair to myself, she and I had just been friends. I'd had no idea that what happened between us was going to happen.

Not until she'd confessed the night before she'd left, after the little going away thing that I'd insisted she have, that she'd never had sex before and wished that our relationship was different because then she could have that moment with me. I could be her first.

What she hadn't known was that I'd wanted her all fucking year.

"That could've been part of it." I pulled her to a stop and stepped in front of her so she couldn't avoid looking at me so easily. "I'm also glad I could actually give you something worth remembering."

The way her face broke into a smile and the sound of her laughter warmed my fucking blood. This woman... She did something to me. And fuck, I wished things were different between us.

I still thought about that night, but in a different way because now I was a grown man and couldn't let myself think of a seventeen-year-old young woman that way. Except when I thought about it now, she wasn't seventeen. She was the woman standing before me.

Once she composed herself, she said, "Both times were worth remembering."

I groaned. "It had to be both times."

"That's what you said. I would've been happy with the first time, but I did really enjoy the second."

We'd had sex twice that night because it had been required. The first time had been... less than ideal and I couldn't let her go home like that.

"Listen," I told her, "the first time, I'd taken so long with foreplay—"

"Which I appreciated."

"Right. But I'd taken so long to make sure you were ready and it'd be good for you that I got so worked up that thirty seconds inside you and I was coming like a twelve year old. I couldn't stop it."

She shrugged. "I take that as a compliment."

"You should, but I had to give you a better memory than that."

Her smile softened. "That's what you said that

night. You said *I have to send you home with something better to remember.*"

"It was true."

The two of us stood there looking into each other's eyes and luckily, I wasn't standing too close. Otherwise, she'd be able to feel the raging hard-on I had going for her.

And that wouldn't be too friendly.

The two of us walked on the beach for a while longer, talking about what we'd been doing since we'd last seen each other. Until she yawned widely. Then I knew it was time to get her home.

It took all the restraint that I had not to go into that hotel with her.

She hadn't invited me and that was a good thing. If she had, I didn't think I'd be able to say *no* and keep our friendship as it was.

8

THATCHER

It was too fucking early to be on an airplane back to Atlanta where we'd left our bus. This time change was going to be brutal.

Most of it was because it had taken me forever to fall asleep last night. I couldn't get Modestie out of my mind. The way she'd looked at the gala and on the beach... It had been unforgettable.

Now I had to pretend that she was my girl around everyone. Most likely, after enough time, the guys wouldn't buy it. We'd known each other too long. They were going to see through it. Which was why I'd decided to talk to Modestie as soon as she got to Atlanta tomorrow. Though I wished she could've come with us today, she couldn't because she had a meeting with her asshole agent this morning, so she'd be at the venue tomorrow afternoon.

"Why do you look so grumpy?" Becca asked when she turned in her seat in front of me. Her blonde hair was pulled up into a bun and her brown eyes were searching for answers. Becca was Lilah's assistant, but she'd become a friend over the months that the two of them had been working for us.

Sean chartered a plane so we didn't have to deal with people and he was meeting us separately. I had no idea what he did when he wasn't managing us.

"I'm not grumpy," I told her, but I kept looking out the window.

Before she could answer, Jamison dropped into the seat next to me. "He's sulking because now that he's got a woman, he hates *being apart*." He said the last part like he was trying to imitate a teenage girl.

"Fuck off." I sighed and hoped the two of them would go away because I didn't want them to know that I really was thinking about Modestie.

"I can't believe I'm going to meet Modestie Dubois," Becca said with too much excitement.

I scowled. "Can you try not to act starstruck?"

Becca shrugged. "I can't make any promises. She's Modestie Dubois. She's beautiful and talented and why is she with you?"

I pushed my middle finger close to her face while Jamison roared beside me. "You know," he told her, "I've been asking myself the same thing. I mean, they were friends in high school. He probably could've had her then, but they were only friends." He paused to consider me for a moment. "Or so they say."

I made sure my face didn't give anything away.

"You all knew her, right?" Becca asked.

"We did," Jamison told her. "And she was great. Still is great, I'm sure, but she had zero interest in any of us. Mostly, I assumed she was a lesbian because she didn't date any guys the year she was there."

Becca groaned and slapped a hand over her face. "I'm not interested in any of you and I'm not a lesbian, Jamison. Maybe you guys are just revolting."

He gave her a wide, cocky grin then flicked her nose with his index finger the way he used to do to Avalon. She hated it, too. "There are millions of women who would disagree."

"Millions of women can have the wrong opinion."

I tuned the two of them out, just happy they'd gotten off the subject of Modestie and me.

Once we were at the hotel where we were staying tonight before our show tomorrow, we had a little meeting as we usually did after a break. Mostly, it was to remind everyone where we were headed in the next few weeks and all of that.

This time, though, once Sean arrived, we talked to him about getting another bus since Modestie was joining us and not a single person looked forward to ten people on our bus. It could technically fit us all, but we'd be tripping all over ourselves.

Jamison immediately asked to be on whatever bus Avalon and Lennox weren't. He'd come to accept their relationship and even seemed happy that his sister was with someone he knew wouldn't hurt her. That didn't mean he wanted to hear it and let's be real. On the bus, you sometimes heard things you didn't want to.

Sean said he'd get it worked out before we left after the show tomorrow.

Avalon, Lennox, Modestie, me, London, and Charlotte would be on one bus. Given that Avalon and Charlotte went back home every once in a while, or said they were going to, it'd be fine.

Lilah, Grayson, Becca, and Jamison would be on the other bus. More room for Jamison to do his thing, I supposed.

Whatever. I didn't care as long as we weren't going to be tripping all over each other.

Sean and his assistant would take care of it.

His assistant, Vanessa, didn't stay on tour the entire time. Actually, this was the first time she'd be here this tour. And she was only here a few days to work on some things with Sean, then she'd be heading back to L.A. She was tall. Leggy with dark-brown hair and eyes. I'd heard her say she was half-Mexican, which gave her a nice deep brown skin tone.

The band knew her, of course, but we didn't deal with her much. She was Sean's assistant and took care of his shit back home while we were on the road.

Everyone kind of kept to themselves that night, probably because we all knew it was our last night to relax for a while.

I called Modestie to see when she was getting in tomorrow.

Her beautiful face filled my screen on the second ring. Modestie always looked like she was smiling slightly, the way the corners of her mouth turned up.

"When is your plane getting in?" I asked after our greetings.

"Um..." She glanced to her right.

Then another voice said, "Lands at three o'clock local time."

Modestie looked back at the phone. "Did you hear that?"

I nodded but hated that time. There was no way I could go to meet her at the airport. We had sound-check and since we'd been gone a while, everything needed to be calibrated. "Who was that?"

"Oh. My personal assistant and overall best friend, Margot." She turned the camera on a woman with purple hair and a kind smile. But it was the kind of smile that she'd also wear while cutting your throat. Or that was my impression of her.

We both said *hello* before Modestie turned the camera back to her. "She runs my life," she told me as Margot muttered, "If only."

I didn't know what that meant and I wasn't going to ask. "I can't come to the airport to get you."

"I didn't expect you to, Thatcher. I'll get there fine. As long as I have the address of where you want me to be."

"Then venue," I said quickly. "I'll have Lilah text it to you. But we have to get shit set up for the show tomorrow night. Otherwise, I'd be there."

The background around her was moving, like she was walking around, and when she entered another room then shut the door behind her, I knew she had been. "Thatcher, I don't need you to pick me up. I've been traveling around the world alone since I was fourteen. I'll get there."

"I'd feel better if I could meet you."

"That's sweet and very boyfriend-like. It would look good, but it's totally fine."

My stomach clenched. She thought I was saying this because of the fake relationship thing, but I'd honestly wanted to be there. If we weren't together, we were at least friends.

"All right," I finally told her. "I'll see you tomorrow then."

"Good night, Thatcher." She ended the call without hesitating.

This was the perfect time to remind myself that she wasn't mine. She wouldn't ever be. We'd fake it for a while, but the lines had been drawn and I needed to remember that.

But it was too fucking easy to get lost in Modestie Dubois.

The next day, we got right back into the swing of things and before I knew it, Sean came into the dressing room to get me.

"Modestie's here," he told me. I looked behind him and didn't see anyone.

"Where is she?"

"She asked me to come get you," was all he

told me.

Furrowing my brows as I hopped up from the chair, I didn't understand why she hadn't just come in with him. Still, I followed him until he pointed to the exit.

She was outside?

Pushing into the midafternoon sunlight, I didn't see her at first. She'd tucked herself behind the door. I could've fucking crushed her.

She was a sight for sore eyes, even though I'd just seen her two days ago in L.A.

Modestie had her hair in waves over her shoulders and she was wearing jean shorts that purposely looked like they'd been cut off jeans and a white tank top. She had those big sunglasses covering her eyes and didn't look like she'd just gotten off a plane.

"What're you doing back here?" I asked as I walked closer.

"I wasn't sure how you wanted to do this." Her fingers tightened on her suitcase handle. "I didn't want to surprise you with people around. I'm not entirely sure how to act."

I raised an eyebrow. "You don't know how to act?"

She bit her lips together to keep from laughing. "Shut up. I meant with you with people around.

They're going to expect things and I know we talked—"

I put a finger over her soft lips. "When other people are around, we'll act like us. But an us who are together. How you'd act with any boyfriend."

Her jaw tightened in such a way that I had questions, but I'd save them for later.

"Let's take your things to the bus, then I'll introduce you to everyone."

She nodded and followed me to the bus as I explained how we'd split into two groups, which made her offer to pay for one since she was the reason we'd done it. That was ridiculous and I told her as much.

On the bus, I gave her the lay of the land and tucked her suitcase into the spare bunk, where I'd put my shit. Then I told her which was mine to sleep in. Since we'd be sleeping next to one another—i.e., spending nights torturing me—I wanted her to know where it was.

Then we headed back inside the venue.

Before we went into the dressing room, I slid her hand into mine and held tightly. We'd better get used to this.

She greeted the guys and Lilah because she already knew them, then I introduced her to Becca,

Avalon, and Charlotte. They were all here right now, so it was better to rip off the Band-Aid.

"I seriously can't believe this guy swindled you into a relationship," Becca said, even though I scowled at her. "I mean he's great, but you're..." She let that hang in the air and I knew exactly what she was saying.

"When I moved to Michigan, Thatcher was my first friend," she told her. "He was the one I knew I could count on. And the other guys by extension."

"I just have to say..." Becca let the words fall out quickly. "That I'm such a big fan. Araya was my idol when I was a teenager."

"That's very kind of you." Modestie smiled like she heard this all the time. She probably did. "She was my idol as well."

"OK," said Becca, "that's all the fangirling I'm going to do because now we're going to be friends and it'd be weird." A wave of chuckles floated over the room. "Have you seen Forever 18 live?"

Modestie shook her head. "Only in the garage years ago and I assure you, they sound very different now."

The women giggled as I tried not laugh myself. We'd been new back then and we definitely sounded different now. We were just better acquainted with our instruments now.

"Then we'll go to the show tonight," Lilah told her. "I'll set out their clothes early and the five of us can go."

"Sean should be able to find us tickets, right?" Avalon asked Lennox.

Lennox told her, "You know we hold tickets for you women at each show."

"Yeah, but *we women* weren't part of this when tickets went on sale."

Jamison groaned. "That's right. The good old days." The women—minus Modestie—gave him a little bit of hell before he held up his hands in surrender. "Fine. Fuck. Sean saves five seats. One for each of us at each show in case any of us need one."

"To bribe some poor unsuspecting woman to sleep with you?" Becca countered.

Jamison snorted then sat back with his cocky grin. "Baby, I don't need to bribe anyone."

Avalon gagged like she was going to throw up, but that just made the whole thing that much funnier.

As the group continued to banter about why we each might want a ticket, Modestie leaned into me as

I wrapped an arm around her shoulders. In my arms was where she was meant to be.

"You all are really like a family," she said so that I was the only one who'd hear her.

"Yeah. We are."

Too soon, the women were pulling Modestie out of the dressing room to get ready for tonight. I did call out that they should feed her, given that she'd been traveling and all that. The band had to do an interview, which was standard, especially when we were in big cities. The radio stations wanted some spots with us as well as some recorded promo for their station.

It was just part of the gig.

But all I could think about was tonight when I'd have Modestie in a small bunk and what the fuck I was going to do with the erection I was inevitably going to have.

9

MODESTIE

"What's it like to have to kiss someone you don't even know?" Becca asked, causing me to choke on the water I'd just taken a drink of.

"What?" I coughed out.

"When you do movies. Like in the Gassar series. You had to kiss Evan McLaughlin—who is dreamy as hell, by the way. But you weren't with him, right?"

Ah, yes. She was talking about the movie.

Lilah and Becca insisted the five of us get some food before the show because Thatcher had suggested it before we'd gotten down the hallway.

"Right. We weren't together. Never have been. Evan is a sweetheart. He was very cognizant of making me comfortable. It did help that he and I had become good friends since we had three movies before that first kiss."

"And before the love scene."

"Yes, exactly. We're still good friends, which in some ways makes it easier while in others, harder. Because this is the guy who would eat too much popcorn with me when my father was away for long periods leaving me alone with the staff. He's also a heartthrob and I know millions of girls would've taken my place in a heartbeat."

"Do you talk about it before?" Avalon asked before taking a bite of her burger.

The girls were very interested in my job and I understood it. Acting was such a weird profession that it was natural to be curious.

As far as kissing someone you didn't know or weren't with, almost everyone has done that. The only difference was that most weren't paid for it.

"We did, yes. Now intimacy coordinators are becoming more common and I think that's fantastic. We didn't have one, so he and I did the job. He knew what my limits were and I knew his. Him being a few years older than me and male meant that the director wouldn't try to push his boundaries the way he would mine." I swallowed, remembering one of the boundaries that was still being pushed to this day. "So when we hit one of mine, he'd refuse. He'd have my back and I had his."

"It sounds like you were lucky that he's such a good friend," Becca told me and I couldn't have agreed more.

"Excuse me," a blonde girl of about seventeen stood next to our table. "I didn't want to interrupt you while you're eating, but my friends say we have to go. Would it be possible to get your autograph?"

It took me a minute to swallow the bit of food I'd taken, but I nodded. Once I'd cleared it, I reached out for the pen she was holding and grabbed a napkin off the table. "What's your name?"

"Madison."

"It's so nice to meet you, Madison." I scribbled my standard message and then signed my name.

"Araya is such a badass and I couldn't imagine anyone else playing her."

"You're very kind." I pulled my phone out of my pocket. "Can we take a selfie?" I asked.

Sometimes when younger girls approached me, I liked to get a picture if I could. Then I'd post on social media, or more realistically, Margot would, about this kickass fan whom I'd met today.

Her eyes widened and she said *yes* with so much excitement that I was glad I did it. She leaned down to me before I could get up. I snapped several pictures so I'd be able to choose the best one then she thanked me and hurried away.

Hopefully, she'd see the photos on Instagram.

"You're a very nice star," Charlotte told me once the girl was gone and I was sending the pics and details of where we were to Margot.

"Fans are the nice ones."

We finished our early dinner then headed to the venue to get ready for the show.

I hadn't been to a concert before. This would be my first one.

My father had a lot of rules when I'd been a teenager and once an adult, I'd never gone because I worried about being too recognizable. Or that pictures would get out that would anger my father and Brian, which happened anyway and not at a concert.

Lilah and Becca filed into our second row, middle seats with me behind them and Avalon and Charlotte after. It was like they'd planned to have a couple of them on each side of me and maybe they had. Either way, I appreciated it.

The show... I couldn't explain how amazing it was. Thatcher hadn't been kidding when he'd said they sounded different live now. They'd been great when we'd been in high school, but now... Their recordings didn't do them justice.

The five of us laughed and danced through the show. It was honestly the most relaxed I'd been since... I didn't know when. Even my sabbatical hadn't been as relaxing as I'd wished, given that I'd still had the calls and emails from my dad and Brian.

I was going to have to do something about Brian soon.

After the show, Lilah and Becca had work to do, so Avalon, Charlotte, and I went back to our bus to wait for the guys. They explained that the band had a quick meet and greet and always showered before they came back.

We spent our time going over the way things worked on the road. Or the way they'd seen it, since neither of them had been on tour for super long.

Then it was a waiting game.

In one night, I'd made four really good friends. That had never happened to me before.

It wasn't long before the guys climbed on the bus. Lennox and Avalon went to bed right away and given the looks on their faces, I didn't think it was to sleep. Then London and Charlotte did the same thing, leaving Thatcher and me alone in the living area.

"Does the bus just leave?" I asked because I still didn't know how everything worked.

"Yeah. Once we're all out of the venue and it's confirmed we're on our buses, we pull out for the next city. Sometimes it's not long of a drive, so the driver will wait and get some sleep, but we go to sleep and wake up in another city, usually."

His normally well-kempt hair was still damp from his shower and he was wearing different jeans as well as a different T-shirt than he had been wearing earlier.

"How was today?" he asked as he sat beside me and rested his arm along the back of the sofa.

"It was so nice. Those girls act like I'm already their friend. Already one of them."

"You are." He cleared his throat. "At least my friends chose their women well. They aren't annoying and controlling or any of that."

"I hope I'm not, either," I told him seriously, but I chuckled.

"I'm not worried."

"I did want to tell you something, though." I turned on the sofa so that I was facing him. "When we were at the Carlisle Gala, I went to use the restroom and Anison kind of cornered me again." Red anger flared on his face. I put my hands on his leg in hopes of calming him down. "It wasn't a big deal, but I also don't want you to be blindsided by anything. He made his pitch about the damn movie and I rejected it again. He said now that I have a boyfriend, he guesses he'll have to wait his turn for me to be free again. Then he walked away."

He ran a hand over his face and groaned. "I'd like to choke that motherfucker."

"Me too, but see? It's working. He thinks I have a boyfriend, so he didn't do anything too bad."

"He's waiting for us to break up to make another move," he told me because that was what Anison had said.

"I know." I wet my lips then swallowed hard. "I'll deal with that when we decide this is over."

"Maybe that'll be never," he said. I raised my eyes to his. They were dark and brimming, I assumed with anger. "I mean, to keep that fucker out of your life, we might have to be in this for the long haul."

"I can't ask you to do that," I said right away. "But it's working for now. I can get the other parts of my life in order then deal with him. Thank you for doing this."

"It was my idea. Remember?"

I nodded slowly. I remembered clearly. He'd laid it out and this was a fake relationship. Not a real one.

"Let's go to bed," he said. "I'm tired. I think it's the time change or something coming back from L.A."

As if on cue, I yawned widely and covered my mouth with my hand.

After changing in the small bathroom, I waited but noticed that Thatcher was nowhere in sight, which made me think he was in his bunk. When I pulled back the curtain he was.

He was lying there, under a thin blanket with no shirt on, and it was hard not to inspect every inch I could see. He was lean and muscular with so many tattoos that I thought it'd take me years to look at them all. Yet I still wanted to.

"I sleep in my boxers," he told me as I climbed up into the bunk.

The bunks were roomier than I'd thought and since I wasn't very big, I hoped he'd still have enough room to be comfortable. If not, we could make up an excuse for me to sleep in another bunk.

I was wearing a pair of shorts and a tank top sleep set. It was what I usually wore.

We lay there in silence for a few moments, but given how he kept adjusting himself, I knew he wasn't asleep and I knew he wasn't comfortable. So I turned on my side to face him, tucking my hands under my cheek. This would give him a little more room.

"If you can't get comfortable, I'll sleep in another bunk. We can tell everyone that I snore really loudly and you couldn't get to sleep."

He snorted. "Not necessary. I just have to figure out what to do with my one arm." His dark eyes burned into mine, which I could only see due to a dim light coming from somewhere.

"Put your arm wherever you need to," I told him. The muscle in his jaw tightened. "You're doing me a favor, Thatcher, which puts me in your bed. You don't have to try to keep your distance. We're going to touch in the night. It's fine."

His shoulders relaxed like that was something he'd been worried about.

"We should talk about one thing," I said, which brought his attention back to me.

"What's that?"

"Women."

"Women?" He raised an eyebrow.

"Yes. I know the stereotypes about rock stars and stereotypes usually get started because there's some truth in them."

A smile played at the corners of his mouth. "And? Are you asking me if I'm a virgin?"

I rolled my eyes. "No because clearly I know you're not."

"Then what?"

I took a deep breath. "We don't know how long this fake relationship's going to last, right?" I asked. He nodded. "So I want to be clear that if you need to... have a release, I can make myself disappear for the night or a few days or whatever you need."

He furrowed his brows, like he didn't understand what I was saying, even though it felt like I was stabbing myself in the heart by saying it.

"What?"

I sighed. "If you need to get off, I can fly home for a few days to make myself scarce so that you do whatever you need to."

Those shoulders tightened again and through clenched teeth, he asked, "Are you saying that you'll leave so that I can whore myself out?"

"I didn't say it like that, but sure. If that's how you want to put it." I sighed. "I just don't want you having to change your entire life for me."

"Fuck that, Modestie. I'm not doing that."

"I—"

"No. I'm not doing that. I don't want that. Someone would know and it'd get out. I'm not going to do something that makes it look like I'm cheating on you. First, that makes me an asshole and second, I'd never do that to you."

"I didn't mean to offend you," I told him quietly. "I just wanted you to know that I was all right with whatever you needed to do."

"Fine," he spat. "I know. Now let's go to sleep."

"One more thing?"

He groaned but turned back to me.

"I had to tell Margot that this wasn't real. She already started dreaming of the kind of wedding she was going to help plan, so I had to tell her, but I promise she'd die before she spilled any secrets. I had to tell her before I left."

His face softened as he ran one of his hands down the side of my face. "I trust you."

I swallowed hard. "And now that I know everyone here, I don't think we should lie to the people closest to you. Unless you don't want them to know."

Watching Thatcher decide whether or not he wanted to tell everyone that this thing between us was fake was like watching a battle take place on TV. I could see the two sides warring, but I couldn't touch them.

"We can tell them tomorrow," he said at last.

I nodded, then he rolled over and I didn't hear from him again that night.

In the morning, I was awake before anyone else, so I was able to get myself ready without any trouble.

One by one, the rest of the bus woke up to find that we were already at the new venue. Thatcher led me inside to the dressing room, where everyone was, and I knew this was when he was going to tell them not to get attached to me. That I wasn't a real part of all this.

But then I saw her.

The tall, dark-haired woman who'd met Brian's assistant for lunch the day I'd gone in to get the scripts. If she knew his assistant, and if she knew that this wasn't real, there was a serious chance she'd tell her friend.

I couldn't have that. Brian would find out and it would ruin the entire purpose of doing this. The reason I was putting my heart through the ringer would be wasted.

"Can I talk to you?" I asked Thatcher quietly.

He furrowed his brows then followed me out of the room into the hallway. I glanced around before speaking.

"We can't tell them."

Thatcher sighed as if I were exhausting him and

I probably was. "Why not? I thought you didn't want to lie to them now that you're friends."

"That woman in there. With Sean..."

"His assistant, Vanessa."

"I saw her meeting Brian's assistant for lunch that day I went to pick up the scripts."

"So?" he asked like this wasn't monumental news.

"So, if she knows we're not really together, she'll probably tell her friend. It seemed like they were very close when I saw them. Then that means Brian will find out. If Brian finds out, he'll either use it against me to get me to do what he wants or he'll leak it."

"Why would he do that?'

I rubbed my temple with one finger. "I don't think he likes me very much. He likes the paycheck. And I think he'd try to use it as a way to control me. If it's out there, I'll need damage control. I'll need him."

Thatcher grunted and shook his head. "You need to get rid of that fucking guy," he told me as if I didn't already know that.

"I will, but for now..."

"We won't tell them."

I nodded because this was the best option that we had right now. "Are you OK with that?"

Thatcher stepped closer. "It wasn't my idea to tell them remember?"

"Right." I looked up at him through my lashes. "Thank you."

Telling Margot wouldn't prove to be a mistake, but obviously, letting anyone else in on it, would be.

Now Thatcher and I would have to pretend, even when it was just us, like we'd originally planned. When telling those closest to him would've taken away the need to do that.

I was still Thatcher's girlfriend even to the band members and their girlfriends.

And we'd have to act like it.

10

MODESTIE

I lay in this bed for at least an hour after waking up simply because Thatcher's arm was around my waist.

It had always been going to happen. Something was, anyway, since we were sleeping together in tight quarters. This was the third night we'd slept like this, but the first where one of us had forgotten who was in the bunk with us.

I didn't mind it. In fact, having him hold me and pull me tightly against him made me feel all kinds of things. Safe because Thatcher was strong and even as my friend, he wouldn't let anything happen to me if he could help it. Turned the hell on because I could feel his erection against my butt and it'd been a very long time since I'd had sex of any kind.

It just wasn't as easy for women or maybe it was just me. But I had to be careful who I allowed that close because rumors could've killed my career. The guys of Forever 18 could basically do what they wanted and it'd be fine as long as they didn't assault someone and were respectful. The world expected rock stars to sleep around.

They didn't expect that from the girl, who at fifteen, was the chosen one whose only mission in life was to take down the Republic of Gassar and free her people.

It was just the way it was.

Eventually, I had to get up. My bladder wasn't going to allow me to lie there enjoying Thatcher's warm embrace any longer.

Living on this bus was weird, but I was quickly becoming accustomed. I imagined that this was what college dorm life would've been like if I'd actually gone to college.

"Good morning." Charlotte gave me a bright smile, like she'd been awake a lot longer than I had.

I still had my pajamas on—shorts and a tank top —and I'd quickly run my fingers through my hair after using the bathroom, but I wasn't put-together. Now that I took a good look, neither was she. Charlotte and Avalon were at the small table with cups of coffee, but they were still in their PJs and their hair was slightly disheveled like mine.

After the bathroom, I'd grabbed the big manila envelopes that held the scripts Brian hadn't wanted to give me from my bag. I'd been spending the mornings reading them.

"Morning," I greeted back as I grabbed a bottle of water out of the fridge then sat next to Avalon, who was across from Charlotte.

"What're those?" Avalon nodded her chin toward the massive manila envelopes that I'd slid onto the table.

"Scripts that my agent rejected because he wants me to take a role with this director I hate."

"You *hate*?" Charlotte asked. "Is he an asshole?"

I paused for a moment to consider whether or not I could tell these two the truth. Over the past few days, I'd felt like I'd gotten close to them and we'd become friends quickly. Good friends. But the nagging reminder that people will betray you, one that had been drilled into my head since I'd been young, popped up.

They were my friends. Yes. But would they sell me out for enough money? I didn't think so. I'd known the guys when we'd been in high school and it didn't seem that much had changed. Yes. They'd grown up. Matured. But they weren't the types then to be with someone who would do that to anyone.

"You don't have to tell us," Avalon said as they waited for my answer. "We all have our secrets, right?"

"Right," Charlotte added. "I didn't tell anyone that my father is the notorious governor of Michigan until I didn't have a choice."

"'Notorious'?" I asked because I didn't stay up to date on most American politicians, let alone state ones. I didn't live here full-time. I wasn't a citizen, so I didn't have a vote.

Charlotte took a deep breath. "Yes. His family has... a very shady past. A shady enough past that I think it's probably how he got elected and probably how he'll become president one day. He's not overly popular, yet he wins. I don't understand it and I don't vote for him, but there it is. So, to try to make his family legitimate, he went into politics." She took a drink of her coffee and set the cup down carefully. "He thinks that will erase everything from our history. Actually, he wanted to create a dynasty. But my brother decided to be a doctor and I won't touch politics with a ten-foot pole."

"What do you want to be?" I asked.

"I want to run an animal shelter that will never have to turn an animal away." She sighed. "But that takes unlimited funds and—"

"It's lucky she has a rich boyfriend who has rich friends," London said, causing the three of us to jump in our skin.

All three of the guys were coming down the hallway without shirts on. I did my best not to let my eyes linger on Thatcher's chest and strong arms. His lean muscles made that hard to do. He leaned down and kissed the side of my head because that was something a boyfriend would do.

Avalon groaned at Lennox. "With you three here, now she's really not going to tell us about the asshole director."

Thatcher's shoulders tightened.

"No," I assured her. "It's OK. But first, I love animals, Charlotte. I'd love to be involved. Is the rescue operational?"

"Not yet. I'm working on a few things. Getting licenses going. Actually, I have to head home in a few days to look at some places." She blew out a breath. "It's a lot of work and so scary. Some of the possible locations come with a lot of land, which I'd probably need eventually, but it's so much money."

"What'd I tell you?" London asked.

"Find the place, then figure out the money."

"Exactly." He reached out and trailed his fingers down her cheek. It was such an intimate gesture that it almost felt wrong to watch.

I cleared my throat and stared downward. "Well, I'm serious. My mom dedicated her life to helping animals and I'm trying to continue that, so I don't care if it's writing a check or appearing at a fundraiser since I've been known to draw a crowd. I'll do whatever you need."

Charlotte's mouth fell open like she couldn't believe my offer. But it was a real one. "I appreciate that," she told me. "And I'll probably end up taking you up on that offer."

"Please do."

"Now." Avalon shifted in her seat so she was closer to facing me. "What about this director? Do we need to bury a body?"

I snorted. That was how you knew you'd made a friend. If she offered to bury a body with you, you had a friend for life.

"No, thank you," I told her, noticing that my accent was a little heavier now. Just a touch, which no one other than me might notice. I knew the reason. I was slowly letting my facade slip.

My father and Brian had insisted I get rid of my accent to make me more hirable in America. It had worked, obviously, but now that I wasn't paying as close attention, it was starting to creep back in. Though I knew that I could get rid of it in the blink of an eye.

"Then what's the deal? Again. You don't have to tell us." But she wanted to know and there wasn't any reason I shouldn't have been able to tell them.

After glancing over at the guys, I found that they were also listening intently like they wanted the story too. I knew Thatcher already heard it, but I didn't want anyone freaking out.

"He's just an asshole," I told her. "There are a lot of them in the industry." I quickly wet my lips. "But... I auditioned for him when I was seventeen and looking to expand so that Gassar wasn't my only credit. Well..." I swallowed hard. "It was a weird audition. Usually, there are multiple people in the room including casting, but for this, it was only him and me."

Thatcher shifted almost imperceptibly and I had to force myself not to glance over.

"Anyway, I did everything he asked as far as reading went, then he just sat back with this little grin on his face. That's when he made me an offer."

"For the role?" Charlotte asked what everyone was probably thinking.

I nodded. "But there were conditions. One of which was basically that he and I would be having an affair while on set."

"You were seventeen!" Charlotte snapped back as if we didn't all already know this.

"I was," I told her. "He felt that was old enough and that he could... teach me everything that I needed to know."

Thatcher's hand tightened on his bottle of water, causing the plastic to crinkle.

"Is that why he wants you for this new role so badly?" he asked, but his voice was too calm. Most people got scared when someone yelled. I didn't. I worried when they sounded like Thatcher did right now. "He thinks he can do the same thing now?"

I wasn't sure why he was so affected by this story when I'd already told him but I had glossed over some of the details before.

I shrugged. "Probably." Though I knew that absolutely was the reason. "And why he wants to get me naked on screen so badly. He knows I don't want that, but it makes me vulnerable and gives him some control."

"You're not doing it," said Thatcher. It wasn't a

question, but a directive, so I furrowed my brows. I'd already told him this but maybe this was part of the fake relationship thing. Maybe he was pretending that it was all new information.

"Of course I'm not doing it. I've said that at least a dozen times. It's why I'm wading through these awful scripts to find something else that I might like." I indicated the envelopes on the table.

Thatcher's jaw clenched so hard that I thought it might explode before he walked away. Lennox and London gave each other a look then headed back down the hallway without a word.

I gave the girls both a small smile. "Was it something I said?" They giggled and while I would obsess about Thatcher's reaction for a while, I tried my best to remain unaffected.

"I'm sorry some men are such assholes," Avalon told me.

"Thank you. Me too."

The three of us started a new topic. Or rather one we'd already been on.

The scripts.

As I explained each one, they thumbed through the pages, each of us laughing at the ridiculous parts. In this case, Brian wasn't exactly wrong. Most of them were shit. But I was determined to find a diamond in the rough.

After spending the day with the girls and going to dinner with them while the guys did their show, I began to feel worse about lying to them. It was the safe option, but I hated it and had to convince myself that it wasn't wrong since it was what we needed to do to keep the people in my world from knowing the truth.

Still, it was a terrible way to get started in a relationship.

Thatcher and I didn't talk much before we were climbing back into the bunk together that night. I hoped it was more that he was busy than angry because there was no reason for him to be angry with me. I hadn't done anything.

"Are you all right?" I asked him once we were both settled, the slider on the bunk was closed, and the one light in the corner was still on.

"I'm fine."

"You seem like you've been in a mood since this morning," I told him.

"I have been." He took a deep breath. "Because I've wanted to go wring that guy's neck and it intensified this morning."

I furrowed my brows as I turned onto my side to

face him. Thatcher was lying on his back staring at the ceiling. "What guy?"

He immediately turned to look at me like I was insane. "*What guy?* The grown-ass man who wanted to fuck you when you were seventeen in exchange for a role. Ring any bells?"

"Oh." It was all I could say because I'd known he'd been angry when I'd told the girls what had happened, but I hadn't known he'd still be so angry. "I didn't do it."

He groaned and ran a hand over his face. "I wasn't angry with *you*, Modestie. That guy's a fucking predator and I hate that you were in that position or that he's still, after several years, trying to get you in bed."

"It won't work," I assured him. "I made enough money on the series that I could never work again and that would be my choice if the only other one was ever working with Anison Brecht. Why do you think I have you as my big, fake boyfriend?" I asked to try to lighten the mood. "To scare him off."

"I fucking hate it."

"Same. But I can't change or control him. I can only control me and I'll keep putting as much distance between him and me as I can."

"But he's every fucking where."

"He's not here." I smiled up at him, hoping it would alleviate some of his anger. "I don't see him in this bunk." Glancing around, I made a big show of the fact that I was double-checking to make sure he and I were alone in the bunk. "And I'm fairly sure he's not on this bus. He's thousands of miles away from me."

Thatcher seemed to relax with those reassurances, but I knew him and the topic would still always be in the back of his mind. "That's true. I just..."

Then he did something I never could've expected.

Thatcher quickly leaned in and kissed me. His lips pushed against mine, taking me by surprise. One hand cupped my cheek as he propped himself up on the other elbow. He was over me, leaning onto my body, and I would have lied if anyone asked how good it felt.

I'd never admit that I've wanted this since the day I went back to France. That I thought about Thatcher long after we'd lost touch.

It would've been embarrassing.

Because it felt so good to have him there in my space, his body touching mine, his tongue stroking over my lips. But this wasn't a slow kiss. This was hard and demanding. Rough, but not too rough.

This was the kiss I'd been dreaming about, but I knew that it was going to come to an end all too quickly.

11

MODESTIE

"Sorry," he said after pulling back, regret all over his face.

"I really didn't mind." It was the honest answer. "I haven't been kissed like that since..." I wracked my brain trying to figure out when I'd ever been kissed with that much passion and knew the answer. "Ever. Or at least since you."

He snorted and this little grin curved his lips.

Thatcher hadn't moved away from me very far and I could feel his erection pulsing against my thigh. My heart raced at the idea of him kissing me turning him on.

"I shouldn't have done it," he said quietly as he looked down at me. "This thing between us isn't real and I crossed a line."

"A line I didn't mind being crossed," I assured him. When he cocked his head to the side, my skin heated, though I hoped he couldn't see it, given the dim lighting. "It's been a very long time since anyone has touched me that way."

"A kiss?" The disbelief in his voice was clear.

People thought that when you were a celebrity, then the opposite sex fell all over you. Or the same sex. Whatever you were into.

I rolled my eyes and sighed. "Yes, Thatcher. I've been kissed, but not... not like that." And I really didn't want to explain what I meant by that. "Hell, I haven't had an orgasm given by another person since you, even though yes, I've had sex since then. Let's just say that not all men are givers."

His entire face scrunched up, like I'd just said the most ridiculous thing he'd ever heard. "Please tell me you're joking," he said. I shook my head, but now I wanted to melt into the mattress and disappear. He shook his head. "Well, if you ever want help with that, let me know."

I snorted. "Don't threaten me with a good time." This interaction reminded me of some when we'd been in high school before we'd had sex. The sex before I'd left had happened because I'd wanted my first time to be with someone I trusted absolutely and

I'd worried that I wouldn't find that once I wasn't with him.

His eyes darkened as he leaned in. "I'm fucking serious, Modestie. Your orgasm is my command. And you know I'm a diligent worker."

He had been. Actually, it'd been surprising when we'd been together before just how good he'd been at it and how concerned he'd been with making me feel good. I'd heard horror stories from other women and knew that most high school guys weren't usually like that.

Just like then, I didn't want to think about how he'd gotten so good at it or how much more experience he might've had now than he'd had then. Or how much better he'd be at it.

Instead, I swallowed hard and willed my racing heart to stop taking my stomach on the roller coaster ride of its life.

We'd been friends who had sex before. Maybe we could be again.

Slowly, I reached up and traced his chin with my fingers. Then, without giving myself time to talk myself out of it, I pushed my lips against his. Thatcher groaned and pushed back, causing me to lie back on the mattress. He kissed me as his fingers trailed down my arm.

I couldn't believe I'd done that. Couldn't believe we were kissing again and honestly didn't want to hope for what he'd said he'd give me.

I'd given myself enough orgasms over the years to know how to get the job done, but as his fingers pushed past the waistband of my shorts, I knew that this would be different. Me doing it to get off as quickly as possible wasn't going to be the same as what Thatcher would make me feel.

His finger brushed my skin on its way south. He nudged my legs apart and they cooperated, even though I hadn't told them to. Then he touched me. Touched me in a way he hadn't in six years. He was gentle down there as his kisses became more urgent and I pushed away any questions about how I'd look him in the eye when this was done.

I hadn't before. Back then I'd just left and our relationship had consisted of text messages and Face-time calls where I hadn't really been looking at him. Then there'd been nothing.

His finger circled my most sensitive area like he was hellbent on teasing me. He did it again before adding any pressure. A sound caught in my throat when he pushed a finger inside me and my head fell back, breaking that kiss.

He continued to kiss and suck his way down my

neck as he added a second finger. It'd been so long that those two fingers were a little uncomfortable at first, but after three thrusts, I was wet and they slid so easily, bringing me so much pleasure.

But then he pulled them out and the weight of him against me was gone. I was about to open my eyes to see why he'd changed his mind, but I didn't have to. He hadn't changed his mind at all. Right now, he was pulling my shorts and panties down my legs. Once the lower half of me was bare and my legs were spread again, he let out a long, slow sigh that made me open my eyes enough to see what was wrong.

He was staring between my legs and the look on his face wasn't one of something being wrong. It was very much the look of something being right. Thatcher ran his tongue over his bottom lip then carefully worked himself into a position that allowed him to lower his mouth to me and lick.

Every muscle in my body tightened as my fingers curled into the sheet covering the mattress. It took everything in me not to call out in pleasure, but there were other people on this bus and that would make it hard to face them in the morning.

He licked me again and again and I thought he couldn't be comfortable in the position he was in, but he wasn't complaining, so I wouldn't, either. He lifted my leg so that it was over his shoulder. I adjusted myself so that I was turned across the mattress, giving him more space because whatever he wanted to do to me, I wanted him to do.

"Fucking Christ, Modestie." His voice was low and full of desire before he ran his tongue up me again then sucked my clit between his lips.

I nearly came undone right then and there. But instead, I continued to let him work. Thatcher used those magic fingers and that expert tongue to build my orgasm until I couldn't take it anymore.

"Thatcher," I pled.

It must've been the thing he needed because he did this thing with his tongue that had me coming in an instant. He kept sucking until I was slowly falling back down to Earth after what was possibly the greatest ride of my life.

I lay there, staring at the ceiling as I tried to catch my breath, but I was breathing like I'd just run a marathon I hadn't trained for.

How unattractive.

But Thatcher chuckled, which made me glance down in time to see him wipe the back of his hand across his mouth. Embarrassment burned through me at the realization of the reason he'd had to wipe his mouth.

"I..." My breath hadn't come back yet, so I took another and blew it out slowly.

"I love that I can make you breathless."

After a giggle, I said, "You're very good at that. And I'll repay the favor in just one second." I raised a single finger into the air tiredly. "But to warn you, I won't be as good at it."

He fought back a grin. "What?"

Now that I wasn't breathing like a pushed nose pug who'd just had the zoomies, I told him, "I'll repay the favor, but I won't be as good at it. I..." I sighed and shook my head. "I don't have the experience you have."

He furrowed his brows. "Are you talking about sucking my dick?"

I slapped a hand over my face. If there was another thing Thatcher was good at, it was making me blush even when he didn't intend to. "Yes." But it came out more as a groan.

He reached out and pulled my hand away from my face and hovered over me so I didn't have much choice but to look at him.

"Modestie," he said quietly. "If you put my cock in your mouth, I promise you, it'll be fantastic. If you're unsure, I'll teach you, but, woman, it isn't possible you wouldn't be good at it."

I shrugged. "I guess we'll find out."

As I tried to move so he'd lie down, he wouldn't let me by. Instead, he nudged me back down.

"Not tonight, you won't. That was for you and I don't want you doing that because you think you have something to prove. You have nothing to prove. You're beautiful. You're smart. You're sexy as hell. The only problem with you is you seem to have been with men who don't know what the fuck they're doing."

"Man," I corrected.

"What?"

"It was only one person. Not really a relationship, but someone who I'd have sex with once in a while."

He put a finger over my lips to stop me from talking. "Shut the fuck up." His tone was playful, so I didn't take offense. "I don't want to hear about it."

I nodded so he'd remove his finger from my mouth and when he did, I wet my lips. "So you don't want me to..." I let the implication hang in the air.

Thatcher fell back against the mattress with a sigh. "Not tonight," he said quietly and I wasn't exactly sure why.

Tit for tat. Wasn't that the saying? He'd given me something, so I should give him something and that was when I realized how transactional that sounded.

But wasn't that what it was? A transaction between friends?

To prove his point, Thatcher handed me my clothes so that I could get dressed then we were both back under the covers and this weird silence hung between us.

We'd had silence before, but it'd never been uncomfortable. Maybe it was only uncomfortable to me.

"So at a later date?" I asked him.

His deep chuckle filled the air around us. "You don't have to do anything for me, Modestie. That was for you and anytime you need another one, let me know. I'll gladly do the job."

I elbowed him in the shoulder, which only caused him to laugh louder. "Seriously," he continued. "I get we're doing this fake thing, but we're friends, at least. We're in this situation. If you need something, anything, tell me. I'll take care of it."

My heart sputtered for a completely different reason now.

Thatcher didn't have to be like this with me. He was doing me enough of a favor by pretending to be my boyfriend so that the pervy director would leave me alone. He didn't have to take care of me too, but it seemed like he wanted to.

After all, we'd been friends with benefits once. Maybe we could be again.

"If you mean that," I told him, "then the same goes for you. If you're going to take care of me, then we're going to take care of each other."

Thatcher stared at me so long that I wanted to squirm under the attention, but then he finally gave me a quick nod, kissed my cheek, and turned away.

I was left wishing that he would've let me try to bring him at least the smallest bit of the pleasure he'd given me.

But there was always tomorrow.

12

THATCHER

I woke up with Modestie on my mind and my lips, a fucking reminder of the line I'd crossed last night. Or the line she'd let me cross.

But was it even a line if neither of us cared about it being crossed?

Whatever had come over me last night had to be kept under wraps. When she'd said she hadn't had an orgasm from anyone else but herself since me, it had simultaneously made me question who the fuck she'd been with *and* filled me with a male pride that I'd never had before.

There was only one problem with what had happened last night.

I desperately wanted to do it again.

The feel of her lips, her pussy, her body... it was going to be hard concentrating today.

Luckily, not long after I got up, we were in the venue surrounded by people.

Modestie was wearing a pair of cutoff jean shorts and a tank top, which shouldn't have looked so fucking sexy on her, but the shorts left a lot of skin on display without being revealing. She wasn't very tall, but right now, her legs looked like they went on forever.

"Are you even paying attention to me?" Jamison brought me out of some seriously fucked-up fantasies I was having to focus on him.

I winked at Modestie, but said, "Not at all." Her cheeks pinked up in the sweetest way and I had such a hard time believing that a woman who put herself out there on the screen could blush as easily as she did, but I fucking loved it.

"Fucking hell," Jamison said. "You people suck."

The guys and I chuckled while the women continued talking quietly amongst themselves. We were in the dressing room of the latest venue doing what we always did before a show. Fuck around. Tune our instruments. Whatever.

"Now, now." London patted him on the shoulder. "You know we still love you. We just love them more."

Grayson and Lennox chuckled.

"Yeah," Grayson added. "They let us do things to them that you always said *no* to."

"You guys are so gross," Avalon called out from the other side of the room, causing Jamison to cringe.

That was his sister and now he was probably thinking about some of the things she might let Lennox do. Made me glad I didn't have sisters. None of the guys were going to fall for my brothers.

"We need to go out," Jamison said once he'd shaken those thoughts out of his head. "All of us. Well, not all of us. The women can stay behind."

Grayson, London, and Lennox all groaned at the same time.

"What?" Jamison snapped. "All of a sudden you have regular pussy on the bus and you don't want to go out anymore."

"Jesus Christ," London muttered as he shook his head.

"First," Lennox told him, "don't say it like that. Second, we'll fucking go out with you, so stop being a whiny fucking bitch about it."

Jamison gave us a cocky grin. "Thanks."

I knew that look. Every word he'd said was on purpose to get us to respond. And we did.

We were idiots who now had to go out with Jamison.

The women laughed as they left to get food together, leaving my bandmates and me alone in the dressing room. Sean needed to go over some things, so we were eating here and once our food arrived, we headed to the catering room. We just weren't eating catering. But they had tables and chairs so we could all sit comfortably.

Sean started out with some standard things that we had to talk about once in a while. Offers came in every day. Some Sean would reject immediately. The ones he thought might be worth something, he brought to us. We also had to keep planning new music and schedule recording a new album. There were a lot of moving parts when it came to being a known band and these days just happened.

Once the meeting part was over, the six of us continued chatting and eating. That was when Lennox began to ask the questions that I knew I'd face at some point.

"Did you already know about the director?" he asked.

My muscles tightened because I hated any mention of that fucker.

"Yeah," I said at the same time Jamison asked, "What director?"

That meant that I had to fill everyone in on what Lennox and London had heard yesterday.

"And you haven't killed him yet?" Grayson asked. "That's restraint."

I shrugged. "I figured going to prison would set the band back."

Gray snorted. "Yeah. Sure. That's the reason."

I sighed and set my fork down. "She doesn't want me to do anything. Thinks that us being together will be enough to keep him away. At least for now."

"Is he obsessed with her?" London asked.

"Sounds like it," Sean said, commenting for the first time since we'd switched subjects. "It's not unheard of."

"I know." We all knew the dangers of being in the public eye. But fuck. That man had been jonesing for her for six years. You'd think he'd let it go. "Worst of all is her fucking agent. He thinks this is the only role for her. That's why she has those scripts. Her agent rejected them without telling her so she'd feel the pressure to take the fucker's movie."

"That's messed up," Jamison said before putting a big bite in his mouth.

It *was* messed up and if I had my way, Modestie would be far from that fucking agent, but I didn't run her life. Hell, I didn't even get a say because we weren't together.

"Personally," I told them, "I think she needs a new agent. This guy is a friend of her father's. She and her father don't get along well and I don't think either of them is looking out for her best interest."

"It doesn't sound like they are." Sean took a drink of whatever he had in his cup. It was usually water, but once in a while, he'd indulge in a pop. "If she decided to ditch him, I know people. I can help her find a new agent who will actually look out for her and will work to keep shitty people away from her. As her current agent should be but clearly isn't."

"You know acting agents?" Jamison cocked his head to the side.

"I know a lot of people, Jamison. But yeah. I know a few good ones. Excellent, even. And yes, they're successful. I wouldn't suggest Modestie hire someone who wasn't in her league because she's already a star and probably more in demand than she thinks, given that her agent doesn't seem to want her to know things."

"See? That pissed me off." I set my water on the table harder than I'd intended to. "Her fucking agent doesn't even get her name right."

Sean narrowed his eyes. "What do you mean?"

"I mean, he's been representing her since she was, like, fourteen or fifteen and to this day still calls her 'Modesty.' He doesn't even try."

He shook his head. "That doesn't even make sense, given that she's how he makes his money. Sure, he probably has other clients, but I'd bet my left nut that they aren't as successful as she is. Sounds like she really needs to get away."

"Why the left nut?" Lennox asked, which had nothing to do with the topic at hand.

"I use the right one more." Then Sean got up, taking his trash with him, leaving us all laughing loudly.

But now I really wanted to find Modestie to talk about her agent and everything Sean had said.

"You're not pussing out on tonight, are you?" Jamison called as I headed out of the room.

I raised a middle finger over my shoulder and that was all the answer he was going to get.

The promise to go out with him tonight wasn't one I'd break because he wasn't completely wrong. Given that the dynamic of people's relationships had changed, it'd changed the group too and we needed to have some bonding time. We all needed to go.

It would just be different.

When I got outside, the women were walking through the parking lot toward the venue, but I met them before they got there.

Modestie had her hair up in a bun that was supposed to look messy but was so well put-together that it had to be on purpose. She was also wearing those sexy cutoff shorts and tank top, which I was beginning to think was her signature look. The large sunglasses covered a fair amount of her face, probably to keep too many people from recognizing her.

She didn't mind being stopped by fans, but when she was with us, I'd seen it make her uncomfortable. Like she hadn't wanted to interrupt what we'd had going on, but we got stopped too and she didn't need to worry about that.

"How was your meeting?" she asked as I got to her. The others kept walking after telling Modestie that they'd see her later.

"Fine. It was just shit Sean needed to go over with us. You know how it is."

She sighed then began walking toward the venue again, though this time much slower. "Actually, I don't think I do. Brian doesn't talk to me about much except the roles he wants me to take. I always figured there were things that he talked to my dad about, but never me." She wet her lips quickly. "I think he still does talk to my dad about it, even though I've made it clear that my father has no say in my career anymore."

"That's actually what I wanted to talk to you about."

That got her to stop, turn to me, and push her sunglasses onto her head. When Modestie looked up at me the way she was right now, she looked so damn young. No. *Innocent* was the better word. Like she was curious, sure. But she also looked at me like I had her full trust, which was something I'd never break.

"What do you mean?"

I folded my arms over my chest to keep from reaching out and taking her in my arms. No one else was around, so I wouldn't have an excuse and I didn't want to cross any boundary of hers. We'd agreed to contact if the others were around. Then there'd been last night in my bunk, but... I didn't know what was going on, honestly.

"Thatcher?" One corner of her mouth was raised slightly, like there was some humor to all this.

"Right." I took a deep breath to explain. "Sean

said he knows a few good agents. Successful ones. If you want to fire Brian."

She furrowed her brows. "You were discussing my career with your manager?'

I shook my head. "Lennox and London were asking questions based on what you told us yesterday. Then I had to explain it because the others had no idea what we were talking about. That was when Sean made the offer. If you want to look for a new agent, he'll help you find a good one who will look out for you."

"That's... nice of him." She still looked confused and right then, I wished her father and the agent were in front of me because this was like she didn't understand why someone would help her find the right person for her. Not the right person for her father. "Why would he want to help me?"

I took a step closer and reached out to set my hand on her upper arm. "He knows you're important to me."

She nodded quickly. "Because he thinks we're together."

"No. Because together or not, you're important to me, Modestie. You always have been and always will be."

"I'll think about it." Her tone was uncharacteristically curt.

"What do you mean? Are you thinking about staying with him?"

She shrugged. "He did get me a very good contract for the Gassar series. I just don't want to rush into anything."

"Yeah, but he's also trying to whore you out to a director who wanted you when you were underage."

She snapped back. "That's a really disgusting way to put it."

"But it's the truth." I shook my head and stepped back. "I can't believe you're thinking about staying with him."

"It's not that," she said quietly. "I just can't make a snap decision. I'm happy to speak with Sean and see who he's talking about, but I can't go from Brian Delgado to someone just starting out. Not when I'm trying to break into something new."

"Sean said these aren't new people."

"OK. Then it shouldn't be a big deal for me to talk to him without agreeing to fire my agent first. This kind of change needs to be well choreographed."

"Did your dad know?" I asked.

"What?"

"Did your dad know that Brecht wanted to fuck you when you were seventeen?"

She winced, like my words were a physical touch that she didn't enjoy. "Yes. He said it was all part of the industry."

My stomach churned, threatening to spew anything I'd eaten today. Add that fucker to my wish I could kill list.

"Did he have a talk with the guy? Put the fear of God into him? Anything?"

Her jaw set because she could see my point. She had to. "Not that I know of."

"Did your agent?" I asked. She shook her head quickly. "And he's still encouraging you to take another role with him. One you've been clear you don't want? That's not looking out for you, Modestie. He can't even get your fucking name right, for shit's sake. Not to mention, he's keeping you from the roles you might want for what *he* wants. That's fucked up."

"I know it's fucked up, Thatcher," she yelled. "I've lived it since I was fourteen. But change is hard. It's scary. What if I make the wrong choice?"

Wait. That couldn't be it. She couldn't be too afraid to hire a new agent because change was scary.

"I know." I moved closer and cupped her face gently in the hope of physically reassuring her.

Her eyes filled with tears that I didn't think she was going to let fall and she swallowed hard. "I've never done this alone. My father set everything up originally and nothing's changed."

"You're not alone," I told her quietly. "You're not alone. You can make this switch. I've got your back and Sean knows the entertainment business. He'll look out for you, but I know you could do this on your own. Change is scary, but you don't have to do it alone."

There was so much more I meant by that than just her career. But we were friends, now with an added benefit after last night, but I'd have her back no matter what.

"I'll talk to Sean," she told me so quietly that I almost didn't hear her.

After a quick kiss to her forehead, I wrapped my arm around her shoulders and led

her into the venue.

If I had to go out with Jamison and the guys tonight, I was going to spend every moment with her that I could until then.

13

——————

MODESTIE

Thatcher hadn't been in the bunk when I woke up this morning, which should've made me worry. However, the bus had moved and I felt relatively sure that they wouldn't have left without him. He was a member of the band and forgetting him seemed like it would've been a huge problem.

Still, he wasn't there.

And he wasn't anywhere on the bus, at least that I could see.

"Why wouldn't they go out tonight instead of last night?" Charlotte asked Avalon as I came into the room. Both of them were ready for the day and while I'd gotten dressed, I hadn't done my hair or makeup yet.

"That's not a serious question, is it?" Avalon

asked, but Charlotte nodded. "We're staying in a hotel tonight because they've got the back-to-back shows here."

"And?" Charlotte was asking the questions I was thinking.

Staying in a hotel would've made it easier for them to go out and do whatever they wanted because they wouldn't need to be back by a certain time. Though they must've been late since we were still traveling.

"Oh, my sweet, summer child," Avalon said in a sweet voice. "The guys think with their dicks a lot. Like *a lot*, a lot. So having their girl in a hotel room where there's a bed, the only place he's going to want to be is balls deep."

Charlotte slapped a hand over her face before groaning and I couldn't help my laughter. But Avalon wasn't wrong. The guys with girlfriends probably would want to spend the night with them. I hadn't thought of it, either.

One of the bunks that nobody used opened then and Thatcher fell out, his feet landing on the floor with a muted thump. The three of us watched as he came our way.

"Good morning," he said, but it didn't sound like he'd been drinking last night. His voice was deep from sleep but not the way it would've been if he was hungover.

"Morning." I watched as he reached into the fridge for a bottle of water and drained half of it. He didn't have a shirt on and was standing there in just his boxer briefs.

"Why were you in that bunk?" Charlotte asked. I couldn't see her face because I was watching Thatcher and waiting for his answer.

"We got in pretty late." He didn't take his eyes off me. "Didn't want to wake Modestie."

"It would've been fine," I told him as if it were only the two of us in the room and we didn't have an audience watching us.

"I wish Lennox cared about waking me up," Avalon muttered.

"No, you don't." Charlotte giggled.

"Yeah. You're right."

"We were just really late. In fact, I'm going to go back to bed in my own bunk." He turned then disappeared behind another curtain.

Though I believed what he'd said, that didn't stop the trickle of doubt... or maybe it was jealousy over the fact that there could've been another reason he hadn't wanted to sleep with me.

If he'd been out and hooked up with someone, as

was his right since we weren't together, he might not have wanted to climb in with me until after he took a shower.

Oh, man. I hated that idea. Fear gripped my stomach when I thought that might've been what had happened. But I didn't know, so I shouldn't have gone there without talking to him first. Even still, I couldn't be mad if he had done it.

Sex was something the guys were used to and Thatcher couldn't have it because I was here. Plus, I'd told him he could. That I'd make myself disappear so he could have his needs met.

I'd have to ask him as soon as I got a chance because the last thing I wanted was to be blindsided. Even if his sex life was technically none of my business.

There wasn't a chance to talk to him until after the show. While the guys did what they needed to do, Lilah, Becca, Charlotte, Avalon, and I got settled into the hotel. We'd brought our respective guys' bags with us too because Lilah said that was what they did.

The five of us hung out together until the guys were done. Then we all went our separate ways. The show had been a little earlier today, so when the guys got to the hotel, there was still plenty of night left.

"What do you feel like doing tonight?" Thatcher asked as he looked for something in his duffle bag. He didn't tell me what he needed or I might've been able to lead him right to it.

"I don't really care," I told him. I hesitated. "That's not one hundred percent true. I don't really feel like going out if that's what you were thinking. But you know you don't need to babysit me. You can go out if you want."

"Nah." He shook his head. "What sounds good to me is a nice, long soak in the hot tub, then room service. Just a chill night."

"That does sound good."

"Then you'd better get changed."

After finding my red bikini, I hurried into the bathroom to change and put my hair up. If we were going in the hot tub, I really didn't want to get the chlorine in my hair. Not tonight. I could shower off my body, but washing my hair was more effort than I wanted to make.

I had a beautiful, black coverup that fastened in the middle just under my breasts that I had also put on because I didn't want to be running around the hotel in just a bikini. Then I slid on some flip-flops that I used for this kind of thing and was ready to go.

Thatcher had put on swim trunks and a T-shirt along with his shoes then led me up to the hot tub.

At this hotel, the pool and hot tub were on the roof. They were enclosed with glass walls on three sides and a glass ceiling, giving us a fantastic view of the city.

The two of us shucked off all the unnecessary clothing then slowly lowered ourselves into the hot tub. It wasn't huge, but it definitely would've fit more people. Though right now, it was empty.

"Wait. It's ten o'clock. Aren't they closed?" I asked once we were both fully in. The water came up to Thatcher's chest as he relaxed back with his arms on the sides.

"Yeah. I talked to them. Don't worry." He closed his eyes and dropped his head back.

"What does that mean?"

"I asked if we could use it even though it's closed. They didn't have a problem with it."

"So we're alone? No one can come in?"

"Yup."

"We could do anything and no one would know?"

Thatcher cracked one eye just enough that he could look at me, then one side of his mouth curled up. "What'd you have in mind?"

Thankfully, the water was hot because the flush of my face could be explained by that, even though it wasn't the water making my skin pink.

"Nothing. I was just asking."

"Then yes. We could do anything. No one's here."

Which also made it a perfect place to ask the question that had been on my mind all day.

"Why didn't you come into the bunk last night?"

He lifted his head and opened his eyes. "I told you why. I didn't want to wake you."

"Is that really all? Because if it's because you hooked up last night and didn't want to sleep next to me while having..." I swallowed hard because the words already felt like acid burning my throat. "Her all over you, you can just tell me. I already told you I'd disappear when you had needs to be met. I can fly home for a few days, even."

His jaw tightened. "You done?" he asked. I nodded. "I didn't do anything with anyone last night. We got back late and I didn't want to wake you up by clumsily climbing over you. I had a couple of drinks, but I wasn't drunk. And I already told you that I'm not going to fuck anyone else while people think we're together. If anyone found out, it'd make me look like a big fucking asshole and make you look like the poor woman whose boyfriend cheated on her. I don't want that for either of us."

"You did say that, but—"

"But nothing. I was with the guys last night. If they thought I was cheating on you, they'd kick my ass. Slowly. With a lot of pain."

Fighting back a smile, I didn't want to admit how much I loved that the guys would protect any one of the girlfriends.

"I just wanted to make sure you knew I was serious."

"I know," he said, sounding exasperated. "I know you're serious, but I don't want anyone while you're with me."

And how damn much I wished he meant that for reasons other than saving us both the embarrassment.

Thatcher had done something for me the other night and I thought I could definitely do something for him. If he wanted me to. Now I wasn't going to do oral right there in the hot tub, no matter whether or not anyone could see us. But I could do... something.

After hyping myself up, I waded over to him and grabbed on to his shoulders so that I could climb into his lap. He held on to my hips as I got myself situated.

"What're you doing?" he asked quietly.

"Paying you back." I slid my hands up to the sides of his face then leaned in and kissed him.

I'd never initiated a kiss in real life ever. It was insanely nerve-wracking. The potential for rejection was almost too much for me to take and I was well used to rejection. I'd been rejected from auditions, by my father's lack of love and affection, but the idea of being rejected by Thatcher was almost more than I could bear thinking about.

"Modestie." My name sounded like a prayer on his lips, but it could've been a warning. I didn't need a warning.

I leaned in and pressed my mouth to his. He needed no coaxing to take over. He slid a hand up my back until he rested on the back of my neck and was able to tilt me the way he wanted me. This reminded me of when we'd been together before. He'd taken control then and he was taking it now. All I could do both times was hang on for the ride.

Thatcher wrapped his other arm around my lower back and pulled me toward him, pressing my sensitive area to his erection.

"What're you doing?" he asked again after bringing the kiss to an end.

"You gave me a fantastic orgasm the other night." I shrugged. "I want to pay you back. You're sacrificing a lot by pretending to be with me."

The muscle in his jaw clenched then released. "You don't owe me anything."

"I knew you'd say that. If you don't want to..." I tried to move away, but he tightened his grip on my body.

"Didn't say that," he told me. "I said you don't owe me anything. I don't want you to feel like you *have* to have sex with me, Modestie. I'm not trying to take advantage of you here. You have enough of that in your life."

I smiled up at him. "I know you're not taking advantage of me, Thatcher. I'm trying to take advantage of you," I said. His chuckle echoed through the empty swim area. "But seriously. We were friends who had sex before, and it didn't hurt our friendship. Why couldn't we do that again?"

Thatcher's gaze remained focused on mine for long enough that I thought he might've forgotten what I was trying to do. Then he nodded. "We can. We don't have to."

"But what if I *want* to, Thatcher? There's very

little that I get to have control of in my life. Maybe this is one thing I want to be able to decide for myself."

Apparently, those words worked because Thatcher grabbed the back of my neck and brought me in for another kiss. His hands slid over all the exposed skin of my shoulders and back. Then they fell to my thighs and stroked there as his tongue danced over mine.

I was a whimpering mess in no time. His fingers moved up the inside of one of my thighs, pausing only momentarily at my bikini bottom before pushing them aside and circling my clit.

My head fell back as a quiet moan escaped. Thatcher really knew how to work me up and it wouldn't be long before I fell off the edge right there in the hot tub. Thank goodness no one else was in there, though if there had been, I didn't think we'd be doing that.

He pushed two fingers inside me as he kissed down my chest, scraping his teeth against my skin. I spread my legs as far as I could to give him enough room to do his thing. And when he got me to that point, the best one, the one that I wanted to last forever, I squeezed him to me as my orgasm flooded my body.

"We need to get back to the room." His voice was full of desire. I could only nod in agreement then follow his lead.

He pulled me up out of the hot tub, led me to the shower they had there so you could wash off the chlorine, then he handed me a towel. After drying ourselves off quickly, I put my coverup back on, then he took my hand and walked to the elevator so quickly that I was taking twice as many steps as I normally would to keep up with him.

We hurried off the elevator when we got to our floor. Thatcher opened the door and pulled me through. After shutting it behind us. He pushed me up against it and kissed me deeply. Thatcher always tasted the same. I didn't know how that was possible, but it was. His kiss was demanding yet so gentle that I wanted to demand more.

Like he could hear my thoughts, he gave me more. More intensity, more... everything. He kept kissing me as he pulled me from the door. Every sense was filled with Thatcher as he unsnapped my coverup, letting it fall to the floor, then quickly untied my bikini. Soon I was naked in the cool room with goosebumps covering me from head to toe.

How he was doing all of this without looking, I'd never know.

Thatcher yanked the covers back on the bed and broke the kiss.

"On the bed."

"But I thought I'd..." I ran my hand over his covered erection so I wouldn't have to say the words and embarrass myself more than I already had.

His fingers circled my wrist and pulled it away. "Not a chance," he said. I raised an eyebrow. "If you even touch me right now, we're going to have a repeat of the first time we had sex." I snickered because that had lasted about thirty seconds and it hadn't been because Thatcher had been a blushing virgin. "I'm not doing that again. We're not doing that again, but I've wanted back inside you for so long that it's exactly what will happen. So on the bed."

His wish was my command. I crawled up and settled back. Thatcher watched me the entire time and I hoped to hell I'd at least done it sexily. He pulled off his own swim trunks, went to his bag, and came back with a condom, then was soon hovering over me. Skin to skin with nothing between us.

I'd started shivering from the cold air, but with him touching and kissing me, I was now warm enough to push the covers off with my feet.

Thatcher kissed and sucked, touched and felt,

everywhere he could reach. His hardness pressed against me and all I wanted was him inside me.

He must've felt it too because he moved back to sit on his heels and slid the condom down his length. He'd already given me an orgasm and now, I just wanted this.

When he pushed inside me, my head fell back and a sigh escaped my lips.

"And that sound is how you know you're doing it right," he murmured against my shoulder.

I dug my nails into his back when he started moving. The feel of him against me and inside me was more than I could take. He knew it too because he leaned to one side to fit his hand between us, pressed my clit, and I was coming all over again.

He slid in and out of me as we kissed again, picking up speed with every passing moment. I wanted to think that I turned him on as much as he did me and he was about to lose himself. I didn't care how long it lasted; I'd already had more than I'd planned when I'd woken up this morning.

I just wanted this moment with him.

"Fuck, Modestie. You feel so fucking good." He ran his hand down my thigh, stopping at my knee to lift it higher.

I squeezed my knees into his side, making him groan as he spilled himself into the condom.

He dropped his head to my shoulder, his breath coming just as quickly as mine before he kissed me softly again. This wasn't like before.

This kiss felt like something else.

Something I couldn't allow myself to hope for.

14

MODESTIE

Having sex with Thatcher Hoffman again might've been the biggest mistake of my life.

We were friends and I was already fighting hard-core feelings for him and last night hadn't helped. At all. It had reminded me of all the reasons that I loved him and I couldn't deny that I loved him. And no, it wasn't the friend kind of love. All I was doing was working my way toward a broken heart like I hadn't seen since I'd gone back to France after high school.

I'd hidden that broken heart so well, too. Thatcher and I had still been talking at that time and being the actress that I was, it had been easy to pretend everything had been just fine. It hadn't been fine. I'd spent a lot of time pining over Thatcher and now I was right back in that position.

But last night had been so good that I didn't regret any of the angst it was going to bring.

Thatcher had kissed me long and deep before he'd left the hotel this morning, a reminder of the things we'd done last night. Three times. We'd had sex three times and slept as late as possible. It also reminded me of the things his tongue had done and just thinking about it made me clench my thighs together.

Ugh. This was going to be hard.

He'd taken his things with him from the hotel and I took mine to the venue, though we didn't go together. He told me to stay and take a long shower since hotels weren't a luxury the band got very often and the water pressure at the venues varied.

So I did. And I enjoyed allowing the hot water to work on all my sore muscles.

The first thing I did back on the bus was call Margot. I'd been ignoring everything in my life since joining the tour and while it hadn't been that long, it was still time to see if there were things that needed my attention. Though she probably would've contacted me if there had been.

I pulled out my laptop and placed the video call to her. She answered almost immediately, which meant she was working, too.

"Hey!" she answered with her big smile. "I thought I'd lost you to the rock star forever."

"Never. You know you're where my heart lies."

She snorted. "Please. I'm going to assume that I wouldn't be able to give you the hot sex of a rock star." To her it was a joke because she knew that this was a fake relationship.

The mention of sex with Thatcher brought a blush to my cheeks. Though before last night, it wouldn't have because there'd been no sex to cause it.

"Anyway... I thought I'd reach out to see if there's anything that needs my attention. I've ignored everything for too long."

She waved her hand at me. "You know I'd let you know if there's something time-sensitive." She pulled out a tablet and began tapping away. Margot carried the mini tablet usually to stay on top of my calendar, which right now, was pretty bare. "There's nothing on your calendar for a while. Which is sad. I really thought you'd be filming something by now."

"Me, too, but Brian has kept everything from me, or mostly everything, to try to force my hand on the Brecht project." Margot pretended to gag at the sound of his name. "I know. So I picked up those scripts and first, there are a lot fewer than I'd hoped.

But also, they really are shit. Brian was doing me a favor by keeping these from me."

"Right." It was the sound of her voice that told me she had more to say on the topic, so I raised an eyebrow and waited patiently. "Listen, I know he's been your agent your entire career, but do you think it's possible that he's keeping the good scripts from you to once again force your hand? If you think Brecht is the only decent storyteller who wants you, then you're going to cave eventually. Or that's what he thinks because I've helped you dress for events so I've seen you naked and while it's amazing, I know you well enough to keep you from agreeing to show the world."

I snickered. Margot had a way with the words, that was for sure. "I'm not going to cave on that. No matter how spectacular the movie is." Then I shook my head because talking about me naked this way was truly uncomfortable.

Avalon and Charlotte climbed onto the bus, which probably should've made me worry that Margot would accidentally say something she shouldn't, but I knew better. Just to be sure, I decided to tell her the girls were there.

"Avalon and Charlotte just arrived," I told her and she nodded knowingly. "Want to meet them?'

"Of course!"

I turned the laptop so that they'd be in the picture and made the introductions. After the normal greetings and banter, including Margot asking them if they're taking care of *her girl*, I turned the camera back on myself.

"As for what you just said," I told Margot, "I not only think it's possible he's keeping the good scripts back, but I'd say he definitely is. Right? Or am I being full of myself to think that there are people out there who want me in their movies?"

"You're not," all three of them said at the same time, making me laugh.

"Well, Thatcher's manager, Sean, offered to introduce me to a couple of agents he knows. Says they're very good and apparently not at all like Brian."

"Hire one," Margot said immediately, reminding me that there had never been any love lost between her and my agent.

"I have to meet them first."

"I know, but anyone would be better than this fucker." A phone began to ring on the other end. "Listen, I have to take this, but get me some names and I'll do the leg work if you want. Also, there is unfortunately an email that you're going to want to see, even though I don't want you to see it. Bye-bye."

The screen went black.

Avalon and Charlotte were chattering on the other side of the bus as I went to my official email to see what Margot was talking about. When I did, I was fuming. At this point, I wished I could get a restraining order against this guy, but the experience of others that I knew had taught me that he hadn't done enough to make that happen.

"What's wrong?" Avalon asked as she and Charlotte slid into the booth on the other side of the table.

"Nothing." It was an automatic answer that I'd been telling people for years, even when there *was* something wrong.

"You're lying," Charlotte said immediately. She was right. I *was* lying.

So I took a deep breath and blew it out. "The director who's been giving me trouble—"

"Anison Brecht," Avalon spit out. "I'll never watch another of his movies."

I gave her a grateful smile before continuing. "Yes. He sent me an email. It's a reminder of who he is, what kind of power he has, and what his vision for my naked body on the screen is."

"What is *wrong* with this guy?" Avalon asked and I knew the answer.

"He's powerful. He's at the top of his profession and he's absolutely not used to being told *no*. Most actresses would fall all over themselves to be in one of his movies."

"But this is gross." Charlotte pulled her lips back in disgust.

"It gets worse." There was no emotion in my words and at this point, I was resigned to the fact that I was going to have to deal with him forever. "He mentions it in the email, though he uses such vague language that he knows if I show someone this it will just read like a job offer. Anyway, he says if I'm uncomfortable with onscreen nudity, we can talk about a body double and some other workarounds, but that he'd like to make sure I understand his vision. We can do it... privately."

"That's so gross." Charlotte reached out, placing her hand on top of mine for comfort. Since coming on this tour, people had been on my side when it came to my career for the first time in my life. Well, besides Margot.

I was about to tell Charlotte exactly that when my phone rang and my shoulder sank after I looked at the ID.

I sighed. "It's Brian," I told them so they'd know why I had to answer and on a whim, I put it on speaker. There was some kind of comfort in knowing that someone else would witness the way he was with me. Then I'd have the reassurance that I wasn't doing the wrong thing in thinking about replacing him.

"Hello," I answered.

Only to be met with, "What the fuck, Modesty?"

I cringed as Avalon's and Charlotte's faces blanched. "What'd I do this time, Brian?" I'd been on tour. I hadn't done anything.

"You've been adamant that you didn't want to do onscreen nudity, which meant turning down the role of a lifetime possibly because of it, then you go do this."

I had to assume that the look of confusion the girls had was mirrored on my own face. I had no idea what he was talking about. "What? You know I'm not going to do nudity, Brian. I don't know what the hell you're—"

"The pictures, Modesty!" Once again, he was getting my name wrong and now he was interrupting me like I was the fifteen-year-old girl he'd originally signed.

And that was partly my fault. I'd let him treat me this way for a long time.

"Brian, I don't know what you're talking about," I yelled back.

"The pictures of you fucking that rock star."

Now, that... wasn't what I'd been expecting.

"What?" I asked again as Avalon turned my laptop toward them and began typing. "The pictures have to be fake Brian. I haven't—" Oh, but I had. Last night. However, we'd been in his hotel room. In private. I thought back through every single detail about that room. The curtains had been closed, so no one, not even with a massive lens, could've gotten pictures. So, yeah. I was safe.

"Brian," I began trying to remain calm. "Whatever it is you think you've seen, you haven't. And can I remind you that you're supposed to be on my side?"

He snorted, like I'd just made a joke. "Fuck that, Modesty. I *am* on your side. You're just not listening to me. Instead of doing a movie with Brecht that could've made your career and he was willing to pay out of his ass for you." I winced. His tone always made it sound much dirtier than it was. "You say *no* to that, just to flash your fucking goodies for the world to see for free."

Still confused, I glanced up at the girls, whose

faces were drawn. Then Avalon turned the laptop toward me and I saw what he was talking about.

The screen was filled with a picture of Thatcher and me in the hot tub last night. I was on his lap, my head was thrown back in obvious ecstasy and it did honestly look like I didn't have anything on. It was the angle and his arm placement. You could see the side of my boob, but none of the bikini.

My heart pounded in my chest and my breath came faster. *Shit.* This wasn't good. I mean, in the grand scheme of scandals, it wasn't that big. I mean, last week, an actor had been arrested for prolific child pornography on his computer. That was worse. But for me, who'd been making a big deal out of not showing my breasts on the screen and keeping my private life private... yikes.

"Brian, I—"

"No." He sounded like he'd gotten closer to the phone. "You listen to me. You're going to stop being a little bitch and take the job with Brecht. I'll handle this bullshit. Blame it on the rock star preying on the innocent and be fucking done with it. But you're doing the Brecht job."

"No, I'm not," I snapped. "I'm not doing the Brecht job and frankly, Brian, you're fired. You no longer represent me."

He chuckled. "We have a contract. You can't do that."

"There's a three-month opt-out clause in our contract. If I don't have an offer within three months of filming ending on the last project, either side can void the contract."

"You have Brecht's offer."

He thought he was so slick. Like I didn't pay attention to what was going on in my own career. He was wrong. "That offer came in four months ago. I haven't had a single offer since then. You probably shouldn't have kept all my other options away from me, then, but you played yourself. So you're fired, Brian. I'll have Margot send over the proper paperwork."

Then I hit the *end* button.

"I've never hung up on him," I said, mostly to myself.

"He deserved it," Charlotte told me and I was thankful that those two were there. "Now about these pictures..."

Her tone was teasing, but it didn't stop me from blushing again. "We're not having sex in that picture," I assured them.

Avalon smiled. "There's *something* going on in it, though, right?"

I shook my head and tried to keep my smile away. There *had* been something going on. That was when Thatcher's fingers had been inside me and given me an earth-shattering orgasm before we'd gone up to the room. But I wasn't telling them that.

Before I had to explain, my phone rang again.

This time, it was my father and while I thought about ignoring it, I knew he'd keep going if I did. But how in the hell did he get this... Brian. Of course my father had this number all along because Brian would've given it to him.

Brian had to have it for work and I'd relied on the fact that they wouldn't ask each other about it. Why wouldn't my agent assume my father had my number when he clearly called sometimes? Only he called the other number.

But this was too big to be routed through Margot, obviously.

"Hello," I answered in English because I honestly didn't consider answering in French.

"Modestie, are you out of your fucking mind?" he yelled in English too, though his accent was very heavy.

"Not that I know of."

And that was when he started yelling at me in French.

"You fired Brian? You have to be out of your mind. He's been looking out for you since you were a kid."

"Yes, but he's also pressuring me to get naked on screen and I don't want to do that."

"So you're going to pretend to be a prude after the pictures of you fucking the rock star got out? Show your fucking tits and get the paycheck."

My mouth dropped open as tears burnt my eyes.

I'd always suspected that my dad was in this more for the money than anything else. He no longer drew a paycheck from me, but that didn't mean Brian didn't cut him in for helping corral and control me. I didn't know their situation, but my own father telling me to show my tits to the world was a bridge too far.

After seeing my face, Charlotte pushed up from the table and hurried off the bus.

I wouldn't want to be here for this, either.

"No. I won't. I won't show anything to anyone I don't want to. I'm not a kid anymore, Dad. You can't tell me what to do. This is my career and my relationship. You stay out of it and try just being my dad for a change."

"Well, with the way you're managing yourself, the best you're going to do is the porn sites. How in the hell could you do that in public?"

"I wasn't in public. We were alone. That's all you

need to know." Tears streamed down my face the way they hadn't in a long time where my father was concerned. I guess part of me had still been hoping we'd work through this weird period and be a family again.

That clearly wasn't going to happen.

"Dad," I continued. *"I can't believe you just said that the best I can do on my own is porn."* I swallowed hard. *"Don't contact me again."*

"Your mother would be so disappointed in how you're acting right now."

Without another word. I ended the call and let myself continue to cry.

Avalon rushed over to me and took me into her arms, letting me wet her shoulder with my tears.

At least until Thatcher burst onto the bus.

15

THATCHER

The guys and I had been fucking around and laughing when Charlotte burst into our dressing room and the look on her face made my fucking heart stop.

London was to her before I could get a word out. "What's wrong?" he asked as he brought her into his arms.

"Nothing is wrong with me." She pushed away from him as her eyes settled on me. "It's Modestie."

"What about Modestie?" I asked as I made my way toward the door. I was going no matter what. I just needed to know where I was going.

"Her agent called and tore her a new one because of some pictures of the two of you from last night that were posted online today."

That doesn't make any sense, I thought as I furrowed my brows. "We didn't go anywhere last night."

Charlotte took a deep breath. "They were taken while you two were in the hot tub at the hotel."

At first, it didn't click because why would pictures of us in the hot tub be an issue? Then I remembered and the blood drained from my face.

"What the fuck did you do in the hot tub?" Jamison asked and I would've expected him to sound like he was giving me shit, but there was actual concern on his face.

"Fuck," I muttered then hurried to the door. "Where is she?"

"When I left, she was on the phone with her dad on the bus." Charlotte took a step toward me but didn't come close. "Her agent said some really awful things to her, Thatcher, and I don't know what her dad said because it was in French, but judging by her face, it was bad. Like really bad."

Without waiting for another second, I left the room and ran down the hall, out the door, and to the bus, knowing that basically everyone would be following me.

I almost pulled the fucking door off the bus to get inside and what I found made my heart clench.

Modestie was in Avalon's arms crying while Avalon rubbed slowly up and down her back to comfort her. They both glanced up at the noise I'd made getting on the bus. Modestie's coppery eyes were sad and tears streaked down her face. Seeing her was like being punched in the gut.

Fuck. My heart dropped to my stomach and I wanted to burn the part of the world that had made her sad, even if I was a part of it.

I made my way over to her. Once I was close enough, Avalon stepped back so that I could get in front of my girl. Even once I had her in my arms, my heart didn't stop racing.

Racing because she was hurting.

And racing because in that moment I realized that I'd referred to her as mine and I wanted her to be.

As I suspected, the rest of the group was there by the door. I looked over and said, "Everybody, out."

Not one of them protested as they filed off the bus and shut the door behind them.

Modestie pressed into my chest with her forearms and her face while I wrapped my arms around her tightly. I let her cry for another minute then knew I couldn't stand it any longer.

Putting room between us was the last thing I

wanted to do, but I also needed to look into her eyes as I spoke.

"You've got to tell me what happened, baby," I told her gently, hoping that what I was imagining was worse than reality.

She swallowed hard and ran a hand under each eye to dry the tears that had been falling, but there were still more threatening to spill.

"You've seen the pictures?" she asked, but I shook my head because I hadn't taken the time to look before getting to her.

She moved over and grabbed her laptop then handed it to me.

Fuck. She was beautiful. But that shouldn't have been my first thought. If this had been a private photo just for us, it would've been very different. Probably I would've used it on nights when she wasn't with me.

But that wasn't what this was. This was an invasion of the privacy we'd thought we'd had.

The look on her face was one I wouldn't ever forget, though.

"These are from last night." I clicked to see the others in the series. It was basically more of the same, but she looked naked and it definitely looked like we were having sex. Which wasn't exactly what we'd been doing.

"Yeah. When you were..."

We both knew what I'd been doing. "Right." I put the computer back down so I could touch her again. "I don't know how these ended up online."

She smiled, but it was still small and sad as I ran my hands up her arms. "I didn't think that you did. I'm sure it was paparazzi or someone who randomly came upon us and jumped at the opportunity to make some money."

"I wish like hell I knew who it was."

"Me too." She sighed then leaned back against the wall and looked up at me. Modestie was a small woman, especially standing next to me, but right now, she looked so beaten down that it took everything that I had to control my anger. "But the pictures aren't why I'm upset."

"No? They're pretty personal."

She nodded and tucked a piece of hair behind her ear. "They are and of course, I hate that they're out there, but..."

"The phone calls?"

"Charlotte told you?"

I shook my head. "Just that those bastards said

some nasty things to you." I leaned down so we were at eye level. "What'd they say, Modestie?"

"It doesn't matter." That was the first sign I had that she didn't want to tell me, which, if I had to guess, meant that it'd been really bad.

"I'd guess my imagination is worse than what happened, so if you don't tell me, I'll have to go with that." Though I wouldn't force her.

She took a deep breath and then wet her lips. "Brian said I shouldn't give away my goodies for free and do the Brecht film. At least get paid for it."

"Are you fucking kidding me? Is he talking about the nudity or fucking Brecht?"

The way she furrowed her brows told me that she wasn't entirely sure. "He only mentioned the nudity but honestly, probably both."

"Jesus-fucking-Christ," I spat.

"I fired him." She kept talking before I could get anything else out. "I fired him. He said I couldn't, but I know my contract and I'm going to have Margot send the paperwork over there. We've had it for a while. Just sitting there signed but not dated. She can put the date in and have a copy sent over. I'm done with him."

"Good. I'm glad about that, but not the straw

that broke the camel's back." I sighed because those pictures were going to be out there forever. There was no way to get them off the internet at this point. At least not that I knew of.

"Yeah. It was due." She gave me a sad smile.

"And your dad?" I asked. "Charlotte said you were on the phone with him when she came to get me."

Tears welled up in her eyes again as she blew out a long breath. "Yeah. That was the donkey kick I hadn't been expecting. He and I have never had the best relationship, though during my acting years that he could control, it was better. Anyway, he's upset about the pictures."

"There's more, right? I don't think you'd be this upset if that was all he'd said."

She shook her head slowly. "No. He said I was going to do the Brecht film and show my tits to the world. I mean why not? Everyone's seen them already."

"You aren't naked in those pictures."

"I know that and you know that, but the world doesn't." She pushed off the wall and began pacing. With each path she made, more fear built up in my stomach. Would this be the thing that made her end the fake relationship that was anything but fake at this point, even if the both of us were lying to ourselves about it?

"Anyway." She stopped just a few steps from me. "He said that without him and Brian plus those pictures, the best I'm going to do is porn. Though you'd think that porn stars have a lot more experience than I do. I don't even know how to give a proper blow job." She threw her hands in the air then dropped onto the couch and hid her face in her palms.

"Modestie," I said quietly as I dropped to my knees in front of her and forced her hands away so I could face her. "I'd like to have a talk with your father one day, but none of that is true. You know it and I know it. I'm pretty sure that you're going to find yourself in high demand now that your gatekeepers are gone. You'll get another agent and have all the roles you want."

"I hope that's true."

"It will be," I promised because I believed it was true. "You'd be highly in demand in porn too if that was what you'd wanted, but that's not the best you're going to do. Fuck those guys. They don't even know you."

"My dad told me that… that my mom would be disappointed in me."

That fucking bastard. Modestie hadn't even gotten to know her mother, so that fucking bastard saying shit like that to her was going to hit her hard.

"You know that's not fucking true," I told her. "You do so much for animals just like your mom did and she'd be proud of you for that. Plus, you're an amazing woman. She'd be so proud of you." There was no way for me to know that. Her mother could've been an asshole like her father was, but I didn't think that was true. And maybe her dad wasn't such an asshole before her mom died, I didn't know. If he was… then I seriously questioned her mother's taste.

"He still said it," she said sadly. "And I have no way of knowing whether or not it's true. I never got to know her."

I cupped her cheek and moved her face so she'd have no choice but to look at me. "I know you, Modestie. And there's no way your mom would be disappointed in you. You need to put those fuckers out of your mind."

She took a deep breath and for the first time since I'd come onto the bus, she looked a little more relaxed. "You're right. *Baise les deux.*"

I gave her a wide grin. "I don't know what that means, but I feel like I agree with it."

Her giggle was the fresh air that I needed. "Fuck them both."

"Ah, yes." I nodded. "I definitely agree with all of that."

Then I pulled her in for a hug, resting my chin on the top of her head, wishing that I could protect her from the world. Because if we were being honest, this wasn't the last time those photos would bite her in the ass. And yes. It would be biting only her. Because nobody was likely to say shit about me, simply due to me being a man.

Any fallout, and shit would fall on her. As long as she'd let me, I'd be there to deflect it all.

"If it helps, my mom is proud of you," I told her as I held her.

She'd met my mom not long after we'd become friends. Modestie was with our group a lot of senior year so of course she'd met some of our families.

"What?" Her voice was muffled against my chest.

"Yeah. I took her with me to see the Gassar movie that came out right after you left. It was an emotional one and my mom cried. When we were leaving, she said, *I'm so proud of that girl.*" I had to clear my throat of emotion before I could continue. "And she's said it after everything she's seen you in since."

Modestie started to cry again and squeeze me tighter. Making her cry more hadn't been my intention at all.

"OK." She pulled back and wiped her face again. "I must look like a mess."

"You're beautiful," I told her because it was true. Yes, there was a light-red rim around her eyes from crying, but most wouldn't even notice it. A little cold water would make her feel better.

"Thank you. That means a lot to me." She leaned in and kissed me softly on the lips. There wasn't much to the kiss, but I felt it everywhere.

It was the first time I thought that there was a chance she might see this whole thing as not being fake the way we'd both said it was going to be. One could only hope, but Modestie had been clear that she couldn't manage a relationship, which was why she wanted this fake one. It took the pressure off, so I wasn't going to be the one to put the pressure back on.

But I fucking wanted to.

Fake girlfriend or not, Modestie carried my heart with her wherever she went and if this thing ended the way we'd said it would, she'd take it with her then too.

"What're you thinking about?" she asked suddenly.

"Nothing. Why?"

"You had such an intense look on your face."

Fuck. Couldn't go around wearing my heart on my damn sleeve. "Oh, that. That was just me remembering what you looked like in those pictures."

She slapped a hand over her face and groaned. "Please don't remind me."

"But I definitely want to be reminded. Might have to print them out and save them for the lonely nights."

She bit her lips together to keep from smiling and shook her head like she was trying to chastise me. "I can't believe you just said that."

"You absolutely can," I countered because it sounded like me to me. "The bad part is you know it's all true."

"*Anyway...*" She drew the word out. "I have to get to work," she said. I furrowed my brows in confusion. "I just fired my agent. I need a new one."

"Oh, right." I stood so that she could too, but I

kept her close by wrapping my arms around her. "Let's see when Sean has time to talk about who he knows and shit."

"That was going to be my next step. I just have to call Margot so she can get the paperwork sent over. All those scripts Brian gave me are shit, so I'll be starting from scratch."

"You're going to find someone great. I know it. Then the jobs will start flowing in."

Modestie went over and shut down her laptop, then took it to the spare bunk where we kept all our shit while she spoke. "I'm going to be picky. For most of my acting years, I was filming almost non-stop, other than the year I was in Michigan, which they only agreed to because of some CGI and effects that were going to take a long time. I'm not doing that again. I want to act. I love to act, but I'm going to pick and choose what I do from now on and I can assure the entire world that I'll never work with Anison Brecht."

"Now that, I can get behind."

I pulled her into my arms again, giving her the biggest, hopefully, most comforting hug that I could.

Everything was going to come together for her, there was no doubt of that.

The only downside was that I'd be helping her

set things up so that she could eventually leave and end this fake relationship that was all too fucking real for me.

16

MODESTIE

Thatcher sent Sean a message to see when he'd be able to meet with me and he said tomorrow after soundcheck would be perfect. He'd have all the information together for me.

That was perfect for me too because I didn't want to go in there looking like a drowned raccoon from all the crying I'd done.

Then I called Margot and explained everything. She was pissed at what happened but over the moon at the fact that I was done with Brian. And probably a little too excited to be sending the paperwork to him.

With that in place, I splashed some cold water on my face then told Thatcher he should go back to whatever he'd been doing when my drama had called him away.

"Fuck that," he replied.

"I'm much better. You can go back to what you were doing."

He sighed as he pinched the bridge of his nose. When he released it, his eyes settled on me. "I'm not going to run off as soon as you're feeling better. Come with me. You can hang out with us. The other girlfriends are in there. You all can hang out while we perform. Then we'll come back together." He took a step closer to me. "I don't want to leave you alone after all that."

"You don't have to babysit me, Thatcher. I'm OK."

He sighed and his jaw tightened. "I'm not trying to babysit you. I want you with me. With all of us and not alone."

Being alone didn't sound too appealing right now anyway. So I nodded. I'd go with him after cleaning myself up a bit more.

Once we were out into the sunlight, I let the stress of all of it go. Brian didn't matter anymore. Neither did my father and I'd block both their numbers before I let them talk to me like that again.

Thatcher walked with his arm hanging loosely

around my shoulders like it was the most natural thing in the world to do. Usually, when we were alone, we didn't do the normal boyfriend/girlfriend things because we weren't that. We were fake. Pretend.

Yes, we'd had sex so sure he'd touched when no one was around but that was different. It was the little PDAs and intimate touches that others could see that we didn't do when we were alone. Those were usually for show.

The opposite of what I wished we were.

Inside, everyone pretended like nothing had happened, even though they'd all, or almost all, witnessed my emotional meltdown on the bus, even if only for a moment.

It wasn't until Avalon and Charlotte had come over that anyone brought it up. "You OK?" asked Charlotte.

I nodded and gave them a genuine smile. "Thank you for being there for me. Both of you. For going to get Thatcher... I needed that."

Charlotte smiled back. "I thought he might be able to help. Now." She clapped her hands together. "What are we doing while they're on stage? I'm spoken for after the show, but I'm yours until then."

"You're never theirs," London called out. I was surprised he could hear us. "You're always mine."

"Yeah, OK, caveman." Then she rolled her eyes where he couldn't see her. "Anyway, what do we want to do? Not go watch them, right? We've done that. They don't need the attention."

The three of us giggled, bringing me right out of the funk my father and Brian had put me in.

I was free. Now I could enjoy it.

Not a single person mentioned the pictures online or what it looked like Thatcher and I had been doing.

The girls and I sat around the bus watching funny videos and laughing like I felt like I hadn't in forever. To think I never would've met them if Anison Brecht hadn't been creepy where Thatcher could see him blew my mind.

That discomfort had brought me to a group of people who felt a lot like I thought a family should have.

Now, whether or not I'd still be part of the group after Thatcher and I "broke up" was another question.

So I asked him that night when we were in the bunk after the show.

"Do you think Lilah, Becca, Avalon, and Charlotte will still want to be friends with me after we *break up?*" I used air quotes around the words.

"What?"

"When the fake dating thing is over. We have to break up, right? Unless you're going to tell them it was all a sham. Do you think they'll hate me? Never want to speak to me?"

He sighed a sound that was a lot of frustration and something else that I couldn't put my finger on. "We'll make it my fault. I'll do something stupid."

I snorted. "No. I'm not going to make you out to be the bad guy. We can make a mutual parting. Like we're both just not into it anymore."

"None of the girls or the guys are going to believe that." I really wished I could figure out what his tone meant. I couldn't even really describe it other than to say it sounded like there was a lot he *wasn't* saying.

"Why not?" I asked quietly as I turned to face him.

He swallowed hard but didn't look at me. "Just... Trust me OK? Jamison has harassed me about you since high school. He's convinced something happened back then that I didn't tell them."

"It did."

"They don't know that. Then when we saw you

on the red carpet at the premiere... He started like he never left off."

"Oh." To me, it sounded like Thatcher was irritated by Jamison's harassment of him. Why I wouldn't know but it either had to be because Jamison was too close to the truth or so far from it that it was irritating. "I'm just curious."

Thatcher finally turned toward me, so I readjusted myself to make room, meaning we were now on our sides facing each other. His hand rested on my hip and we were very close.

"Modestie, they love you. They'll still want to be friends with you as long as they don't think you broke my heart. Because while they love you as a friend, they're my family and I know them. They'll side with me. But we won't do that. Like I said, I'll take the fall."

Shaking my head, I rejected what he had to say immediately. "No. I don't want that. Besides, what would you do?"

"Cheat on you." The answer came too quickly for my liking. As if he'd had it planned all along.

It was the obvious answer. The one thing that the girls would never forgive him for because it would play into any fear they had or could create a little twinge of doubt where there'd only ever been trust.

If my rock star boyfriend could cheat on me, then what was stopping theirs?

"Absolutely not," I told him. "They'd look at you differently. That could put a strain on their relationships. I can't do that. You can't do that."

"We'll figure it out." He was silent for a moment, but his gaze never left mine. "Is this something you're planning soon?"

"No." If I had the guts to be honest, I'd tell him I never want it to end. That would put him in a terrible spot, so I wouldn't do it. "But I can't impede on your life forever."

"This isn't a hardship for me, Modestie."

That was sweet of him, but there had to be an end eventually. He pulled me into his chest and held me until we were both asleep.

In the morning, Thatcher insisted we get breakfast, though it was closer to lunch. Just the two of us, he said.

Thatcher chose a place close to the venue like we normally did. Plus, they had an outdoor patio where we chose to sit. The day was beautiful and warm. My hair was hanging in a loose braid over one shoulder and Thatcher was across from me in his jeans and T-shirt with tattoos running down both arms right to his hands, looking every bit the part of a sexy rock star.

We ordered and were sipping our drinks, lemonade for me, and water for him, talking about nothing. That was the best thing about my relationship with Thatcher. We never needed to be talking about something important. We could just be discussing how beautiful the day was. We didn't need more.

The food hadn't yet arrived when a man approached the table. He looked vaguely familiar, yet I couldn't place him. He was tall but not as tall as Thatcher with blond hair and blue eyes looking like the quarterback next door only with the mass he would've needed to be the quarterback.

"Modestie? Modestie Dubois?" he asked, but not as if he didn't know who I was. This wasn't uncommon. "I saw you over here and while I normally wouldn't do this, I knew I had to shoot my shot."

Thatcher sat up in his chair. "Excuse me?"

It was like the man had only noticed Thatcher there when he'd spoken. "I realize how that sounded, but it's not what I meant. I'm not here to hit on her."

"Then why are you here?" Thatcher had an edge to his voice that nobody could've missed.

"I'm Lucas Wickman. I'm a director."

That was when I realized why I recognized him. He'd won an award at one of the film festivals recently for a movie he'd made. It hadn't been his first movie, but it had been the first to win an award. And if I remembered correctly, his movies tended to do pretty well. They weren't quite indie films, but they were not at all big studio productions, even when he had a studio backing him.

"That's right." I snapped my fingers. "I knew I recognized you. You just won the film festival award."

Thatcher seemed to relax back into his seat a little, but he was still ready to pounce. I could tell by his posture and the way he kept opening and closing his fists.

"OK. Good." He blew out a breath. "I was worried you'd think I was a creeper." He glanced at Thatcher. "Pretty sure he did."

I gave him a smile because I couldn't deny what he'd said. "He's very protective," I told the man. Thatcher snorted. "Why don't you sit for a moment... should I call you Lucas?" Because I did not want to invite him to join us for breakfast. No. This morning was supposed to be for Thatcher and me and now my job was impeding that.

"Yeah. Lucas is good." He pulled a chair over from another table and sat down. "I have this script that I think is amazing and I sent it to your agent but got a rejection pretty much right away. I thought I'd come over here and plead my case."

"Go ahead." Mostly, I wanted to see if this was one of the terrible scripts that Brian had given me, but two minutes into his pitch, I knew I'd never seen it before.

"Wait." I sat up straighter. "I think this is one that my friend Evan mentioned."

"Evan McLaughlin is already attached to the film, but we've been trying to find our leading lady with no luck so far. I'm worried the damn thing isn't going to get made since we can't find the right person." His deep eyes settled on mine. "I'm pretty sure you're her and that's why we haven't been able to cast this thing."

"Me?"

"Yes. I heard you're looking for a rom-com or something different from Gassar but I've heard that you're connected to the new Brecht picture and I know doing another movie with Evan could bring the comparisons but he's perfect for the role."

"I'm not," I told him right away. "I'm not working

with Brecht now or ever. That's a rumor that I'm pretty sure I know who started."

He nodded. "Good. Between you and me..." He again looked over at Thatcher, who'd been really silent through this. "And him, I guess, Brecht is a creep. I don't understand why he's at the top. He bases his movies off of which starlet he currently wants to fuck."

I raised an eyebrow and tried not to donkey laugh because if that didn't describe Brecht, nothing did.

"Oh, shit. Sorry." Lucas swallowed hard and glanced at Thatcher. Thatcher's jaw was set in stone with that last remark and I felt reasonably sure that Lucas's time here was limited. "I'm a little overexcited to see you in Charlotte, North Carolina scouting locations of all things."

"It's fine. I'd love to read the script. I, of course, can't make any promises other than reading it."

"Yeah, of course. I don't carry a copy with me. Especially when here not expecting to run into anyone."

"Email it to me. I'll give you the address, but absolutely *do not* send it to Brian Delgado."

He nodded in understanding, I rattled off the

official email address that Margot managed, then he left.

"I didn't like him," Thatcher told me once Lucas was out of earshot.

I cocked my head to the side. "Why not?"

"I just don't."

My gut told me that it had nothing to do with Lucas as a person. It was about something else, but he wasn't going to tell me. Lucas Wickman was going to be in this business as long as he wanted to be. His movies were good. Great even. He just didn't play the game that Brecht did and for that reason alone I wanted to work with him on something at some point.

After our breakfast where we didn't hurry at all, we headed back to the venue because he needed to do the soundcheck.

Today was exactly what I'd needed and I hoped it was what Thatcher had needed as well. Plus, once he was done, I was going to meet with Sean. Though I didn't think Thatcher was coming with me for that. It wouldn't make sense for him to, given that this was business.

Sean found me in the hallway after soundcheck, as he'd promised.

"Hey, Modestie, you ready?"

"I am." I pushed off the wall and followed him to the door. Thatcher caught my eye and I gave him a smile before Sean and I left the building.

Once we were settled on his bus, which seemed quieter than ours, even when no one was on it, we dove in.

"There are a couple of agents I think would be fantastic." He didn't waste any time jumping in. "I have more to recommend, but these two would be my choice if you were my sister."

The fact that he was treating me like I was his sister filled me with warmth. It really was like finding my family on this tour. Even people I didn't know very well wanted to protect me.

"I appreciate you doing this."

"It's not a problem. You should have the agent who's going to work for you and it doesn't sound like you have that."

"I don't." There was no reason to not be honest. "My father chose Brian for me when I was fourteen and wanted to act. Then he got me the Gassar series a few months later and he's having a lot of trouble readjusting to the fact that he now needs to deal with me and not my father."

"Hasn't he needed to do that for a few years now, though."

I shrugged. "Doesn't mean he actually got that message. I recently put my foot down. And yesterday I fired him, so now I have no one."

"It was probably the best move. I think you can find a better fit." He took a moment, but it wasn't uncomfortable. If I'd known what he was going to say next, it might've been. "I saw the pictures."

Immediately, my gaze averted from him to the table in front of us as my cheeks pinked up again. Of course he'd seen them. I assumed everyone had seen them, but talking about them was another thing.

"I also know the response you got from your agent and that's unacceptable. He should've been trying to figure out how to protect you from that instead of... well, how it went. Thatcher didn't tell me about it. I overheard Charlotte explaining it to the guys when it happened."

"Makes sense. It wasn't like I was going to be able to hide it."

"Listen." He leaned in, folding his hands in front of him. "I hope you don't mind, but I reached out to the site and they've taken it down. That doesn't mean they won't exist because the internet is forever, but I was at least able to do that."

"Really?" My eyes were wide thinking that he'd

done it for me at first, but then I remembered that he was supposed to take care of Thatcher. "Thank you."

He waved his hand at me like it was no big deal. "You're welcome, but it was the right thing to do. No matter what you were doing in those pictures, it was private. They never should've been taken. And you're good for Thatcher."

Hearing that made my heart hurt just a little. He thought I was good for Thatcher, but we weren't even together. Not really.

"Anyway," he said, "let's make a couple of calls together so I can do the introductions."

This was the first time I'd been excited about this part of my career in a long time.

It was the second agent who I felt an instant connection with.

In almost no time, I made the impulsive decision to sign with Gabrielle Pierce. I'd heard of her before and after an hour of talking to her, it was clear she had the same vision I did for my career. I'd never made a decision so quickly.

I also told her about the script for Lucas's film and how excited I was to check it out. She told me to send her the details and a copy of the script. If I liked it, she'd reach out and start making a deal.

She wanted me to like the script first. That was

new. And she didn't scoff at the idea of me saying *no* to any nude scenes. In fact, she said it was the best move for my career.

Now things were falling into place.

Gabi, as she told me to call her, even said there was a call for a streaming show that filmed in the UK that I'd be perfect for, considering that the producer had literally said they were looking for a "Modestie Dubois type." She said she'd be able to get me an offer if I was interested.

Now, TV wasn't my thing, but it was nice to be wanted.

17

THATCHER

"I can't believe I found a new agent already," Modestie told me after the show.

I'd played my best but had been distracted by thoughts of her.

She was going to get a new agent. The guy at lunch clearly wanted her for his movie. All that added up to her leaving soon. She'd have to go home to deal with things. She'd have to leave to shoot things.

That left me with my dick in my hand because we weren't even together at this point. That was going to need to change. Maybe she wouldn't want to be mine and I'd live with that, but I wasn't about to let her go without her knowing how I felt. Not again.

I waited until the next night when we were at a

hotel again. Only this time, I wasn't doing anything in the hot tub with her. Hell, I wasn't going in the hot tub at all.

We had our things settled before the show and Modestie said she was going to be at the hotel the entire time reading the script that guy had sent her. That was fine with me. I could imagine her there while I played and I'd bet that my fantasy of it was a lot different than the reality would be.

Lucas Wickman seemed fine when we'd met him. I'd told Modestie I didn't like him because first of all, he didn't seem to give a shit that I was sitting right there and while I'm not a fucking diva, I don't know... it rubbed me wrong. Second, I wanted to see what Modestie would say. And lastly, that movie was going to put her back with her co-star from the Gassar series. The one she had amazing chemistry with and I didn't know if he was the friend she had sex with sometimes for a while.

It was killing me but I didn't want to ask.

But she was there when I got to the hotel, curled up on the bed with her back against the headboard and her computer on her thighs while she read what was on the screen intently.

"Hey, baby," I said because I'd decided I wasn't

going to try to hide anything from her anymore. Definitely not anything about my feelings.

"Hi." She didn't look up from the screen.

"Good script?" I asked as I yanked my shirt over my head.

That got her attention. Her gaze jumped to my bare chest. "What?" she asked without hiding the fact that she was staring.

"Good script?"

"Oh." She shook her head. "Yes, actually. Excellent. I'd been so focused on doing a rom-com that I didn't even consider going dramatic. This movie would be the breakout I was looking for." She closed the lid on the computer and set it aside. "Or I think it will be and since Evan is the leading man, I'd be very comfortable."

"Evan, huh?" I walked over and pulled a bottle of water out of the minibar.

"He was my costar in the Gassar series."

"I know who he is." They'd been romantic leads in that movie series and had eventually had a PG-13, minimal nudity, sex scene. I'd been jealous of him then. Getting to touch her, even if it hadn't been actually romantic between them, had had me absolutely bursting with the green monster like I was the freaking Incredible Hulk.

But that was ridiculous. Kissing men who looked like they'd stepped off the pages of *GQ Magazine* or some shit was part of her job. Maybe that was what she liked. I didn't fucking know and that killed me too.

"He the friend you used to hook up with?" I hadn't intended to ask but she'd put it out there like a ripe fucking fruit. What choice did I have?

She snorted. "No."

But I made a sound in the back of my throat that probably sounded like I didn't believe her. I did. She had no reason to lie.

"Wait." She sat up straight with a grin on her face. "Are you jealous of Evan? Please tell me you're jealous of Evan."

"Why the fuck do you *want me* to be jealous of that guy?" Though I hadn't yet admitted that I had been.

"I don't know." She pushed up onto her knees. "It'd be kind of hot to have someone like you jealous of anyone. Especially over me."

"Modestie, you know there are probably thousands of men jealous of everyone you talk to."

She shook her head. "It's not the same. Evan's good-looking and all of that and we are friends, but he's not you."

A smile played at the corners of my lips. "What's that supposed to mean? I'm not good looking or we're not friends?"

She slapped my bare chest but I caught her hand and held it there until she pulled away and moved back on the bed. "Evan is good-looking. You're incredibly sexy. Women imagine Evan taking them to fancy restaurants in Paris or something. Women imagine the very dirty things they think you'll do to them." Her cheeks blushed, which I had come to know meant that she was speaking the truth, even if it embarrassed her.

I cocked my head to the side. "'Very dirty things'?"

"You're the sexy, tattooed rock star, Thatcher. Of course you'd do very dirty things to women. Consensually, of course. Are you trying to tell me you haven't?"

That wasn't something I was going to answer. Instead, I stalked over to her, still without my shirt, which did the job of distracting her.

The fact that we were no longer pretending that we weren't going to be having sex was a step in the right direction. Sure, the relationship was supposed to be fake, but the friendship was real and the sex we'd already had was real, too.

She looked up at me with those russet eyes. "Why are you jealous of Evan?" she asked softly.

"I'm not," I said quickly then added, "But I was." I pushed my fingers into her hair as I cupped her cheek. "Because he got to touch you." I trailed my fingers down her cheek, causing her to close her eyes and her breathing to increase. "He got to kiss you and I couldn't. You were half a world away. I'd gotten one taste of you and then you were gone."

She swallowed hard before opening her eyes to peer up at me. "You know that's all fake, right?"

"Looked real to me."

"That's the point. But when it looked like we were having sex, there were so many things between us that there was no feeling there. We didn't have an intimacy coordinator because they weren't really a thing yet but I was underage, so they had to be very careful. Yes, he stroked my arm. But none of the personal parts ever made contact."

"Doesn't matter. He was with you and I wasn't. That was all that mattered."

Modestie reached out and trailed her fingers down my chest and abdomen, causing my dick to harden in my pants. Her touch always had a knack for making me hard. Even before we'd had sex in high school.

It was fucking torture. But the best kind.

"You've stopped me from doing this twice," she said quietly. "Are you going to stop me again? I know it probably won't be great because I have no experience, but..." She looked up at me with those big eyes. "You taught me before. You can teach me again, right?"

Fucking hell. I almost came in my jeans right then.

Somehow, this woman, who didn't seem to understand what she did to me, knew just how to turn me into a fourteen-year-old who had no control over his orgasms.

But right now, I'd cut off my own left nut rather than stop her.

Instead, I flicked the button on my jeans so that the fly would open. There was her answer. She could do anything she wanted to me.

If I wasn't mistaken, Modestie's hands trembled as she lowered the zipper on my jeans. I wasn't about to leave the woman out there on her own, so I placed my hands over hers as we pushed the jeans to the floor. Then the same thing with my boxer briefs until I was tall and proud inches from her mouth.

She wet her bottom lip as she looked at my rock-hard erection.

"Are you trying to kill me?" I asked, my voice sounding deeper with desire.

Her lips curved. "I'm not trying, but if you're saying that I am killing you, I won't apologize."

"Nor should you."

Tentatively, her fingers slid down the smooth skin of my cock then closed around it to stroke me several times as she watched in fascination.

Suddenly, I wanted to know just how much experience she'd had since we'd had sex in high school. She'd told me about the one guy but not what they'd done. But at the same time, I didn't want to think about anyone else touching her in that way. She swallowed hard and as her chest rose and fell quickly, she said, "I'm kind of nervous."

I wrapped my fingers around her wrist to stop what she was doing. "You don't have to do anything, Modestie."

"But I want to," she almost whined. "I want to do this because I want to know what it's like, but also I want to make you feel good the way you do me. I'm just nervous."

"First, you *do* make me feel good. Don't worry about that." I took a deep breath to steady myself because she still had her hand wrapped around me.

"Second, if you want to do this, we're doing it. Take me in your mouth."

Goosebumps covered her chest as her breath caught before she did what I'd told her to.

When she pushed me past those pink lips, I thought my legs were going to give out. She was slow and tentative, but it was fucking heaven.

Modestie let her tongue wrap around me as she got me wet. Her hand still had a grip and followed her mouth as she moved me deeper into her mouth. I couldn't help it. I fisted her hair, causing her to make this sound that shot through me, tightening my spine. I grabbed her other hand to show her to cup my balls and helped set the pace with the one in her hair.

She licked and sucked, only coming up for air a couple of times while I fought for my life trying not to come in her mouth.

"Look at me," I said with a voice I didn't recognize, but it was the wrong move. Seeing her like that, with me in her mouth, was too much for me to handle. "On the bed."

She let me fall from her mouth with a pop then wiped a hand over her chin. This woman was going to be the death of me, but oh, what a way to go.

"But I thought you'd—"

"Not this time. On the bed."

"But eventually?"

"Yes. On the bed." I grabbed a condom from my bag and rolled it down my length, more than ready to sink inside her. But she still had pajamas on.

In a flurry of movement, I got her naked quickly then pressed my body against hers. She was already warm and wet as I explored with my fingers. Usually, I'd make sure she came first, but there wasn't going to be time.

I sunk into her, causing her to sigh, a sound that every woman should make when they're entered. At least I knew I was doing it right.

I kissed her lips as I plunged in before pulling almost all the way out. I threaded my hand into one of hers and kissed anywhere I could reach. But I was reminded that there was clearly a lot she hadn't experienced and as much as I wanted to stay missionary so I could see her, I also wanted to show her everything.

So I pulled out and said, "On your hands and knees." Her eyes widened as a fire was lit within them before she scrambled to do what I'd told her to.

"I've never—"

But she couldn't finish. I thrust into her balls-deep in one motion. She was so fucking tight from this angle that I worried I was hurting her. Her back arched and her head lifted as she moaned, telling me that this wasn't too much.

Still, I was gentle as I fucked her from behind, running my hands over her smooth ass and then up her back until I could fist her hair. She turned to look at me and I knew that was going to be my downfall. Before I came, I reached around to rub her clit. As I did, her moans became louder, though she was clearly trying to hold them back. Still, once I felt her tighten around me and make all the sounds she normally made when she came, I allowed myself to let go.

Modestie's arms were shaking, so I pulled out slowly and helped lay her gently on the bed. "I'll be right back," I told her before giving her a kiss on the shoulder.

Once I was done disposing of the condom, I came back to find her curled up on the bed like she was too exhausted to move. But she did move. She hurried to the bathroom then came back and curled into my side without bothering to put her pajamas back on.

"I've never done that before," she told me quietly.

"Which part?"

She snorted. "Most of it."

She had to mean everything but missionary and I had to wonder what kind of man she'd been with, but I tossed that thought out with the trash. Because fuck, I didn't want her to be with anyone else.

"Was it OK?" she asked me and I knew what she was talking about. "You stopped me twice before, so I worry."

"I stopped you before for *your* benefit. If I'd let you do that, it would've ended then and there. I don't think you understand how much you turn me on just by being in the same room."

She giggled tiredly then nuzzled her cheek against my chest.

There wasn't any time that would be better than this.

"Modestie."

"Mmm."

"No, I need you awake for this."

She turned and propped her head up on my shoulder so that I could see her. "I'm awake."

"I need you to know that I love you."

Her lips parted and her eyes widened. "What?"

"Yeah. I know this whole thing is supposed to be a fake relationship to get the director off your ass, but it was easy for me to agree to because I've been in love with you since I was eighteen years old."

"In... love with me?" It was like she was practicing the words she'd never heard before. Then she shook her head. "What?"

Of all the things I thought could've happened here today, her not understanding what I was saying wasn't a reality I'd thought of.

"I love you, Modestie. I'm in love with you. There's nothing fake on my side of this relationship."

She sat up, using the sheet to cover her chest like I hadn't just seen it all anyway.

"Modestie?"

"This is just really bad timing."

Now I sat up with confusion. "What?"

She turned toward me. "It's really bad timing. I'm trying to get my career back on track. Just hired a new agent. I'm going to have to go back to L.A. at some point."

I put a finger over her mouth to stop her from going any further. "I know all this. Doesn't change anything for me."

She ran a hand down her face. "We're so stupid."

I chuckled. "What?"

"We're so stupid. I've been trying to fight my feelings this whole time. Told myself that you're just being a good friend and to not get attached this way, but I was always attached. I always wanted you. I've always loved you. But here we go pretend—"

I stopped her with a kiss as adrenaline shot through my body at the prospect of her loving me back. She'd said it. She loved me and I felt like the tallest man in the world. Her body melted into mine as I ran my tongue over her lips. We lay back with her hovering over me. Then she climbed on top of me and put my hard cock inside her. It'd gotten hard the moment she'd said she loved me.

Fuck, she felt good, but she hadn't waited for a condom. At that same moment, she realized what she'd done.

"Shit," she said when she pulled back. "I'm sorry. I got carried away."

When she moved to climb off me, I held her hips in place. "Wait a second." My voice was strained with how good she felt. Her warm, velvet pussy squeezing like a fucking glove made just for me.

"No. I should get off. I shouldn't have done that without talking to you first."

"Talk to me now."

She wet her lips. "I'm on birth control," she told me. "I have such limited experience that I shouldn't give you any infections."

"I wasn't worried about either of those things."

Though that sentence surprised even me. I hadn't been worried about getting her pregnant or anything else that could've come from sex without a condom. Not with her.

Did I want to purposely have a baby? Not really. It wasn't something I thought about, but at this moment, a baby with Modestie didn't sound like a bad thing.

"I'm very careful," I told her.

She nodded like she was relieved then moved her hips. "Teach me," she said quietly and I had never wanted to be a teacher more in my life.

While I helped her figure this whole thing out, my brain ran rampant with the things I could teach her, but for now, this was enough.

Modestie was always enough.

18

MODESTIE

"He said he loves me," I told Margot, whispering like it was the biggest secret of my life.

"But I thought this whole thing was fake."

"Yeah. So did I, but according to him, he's had feelings for me since we were teenagers."

I was outside the venue walking in a circle as I spoke with Margot on speakerphone. There was no one around, so I didn't have to hold the phone to my ear, which I hated.

"You love him too, right?" she asked but probably already knew the answer since Margo could read me better than anyone.

"Of course I do."

"Wow. Look at you bagging the hot rock star."

I rolled my eyes. "He wasn't that when I met him. Anyway, did you check out Gabrielle?"

"I did." Some papers shuffled on the other end of the phone. "She checks all the boxes and everything looks good. I couldn't find a single person who had any dirt on her. She sounds like she's the dream."

"Brian was the dream once."

Margot groaned. "Brian was never the fucking dream, Modestie. You only think that because he negotiated the contract for the series. He's long past his expiration date."

"I know. I know." I sighed. "Then I'll move forward with her. Can you take care of things?"

"Sure thing, boss. I'll get the paperwork and have the lawyer look it over. You'll get a copy, then we'll sign and get it back, but she said she'd start looking for things for you before the paperwork is finalized so that you can hit the ground running. She even mentioned something about a streaming drama."

"Yeah. She mentioned that to me too. I'm not sure I want the rigor of a series, though."

"Yeah, I didn't think it was your jam, but you should think about it. Step out of your comfort zone."

"I'll think about it, but I've got to go."

We ended the call and I felt lighter than I had in

years. It was like my entire life was finally falling in line.

I made my way into the venue to go to the dressing room, where I thought everyone probably would be. They were, but when I entered the room, the tension could've been cut with a freaking knife.

The girls were kind of huddled on one side of the corner, but their conversation ended as soon as they saw me. That wasn't a good sign.

Jamison was the only one to greet me while Grayson had his arms crossed, Lennox was rubbing his chin, and London just leaned against the wall near Charlotte.

"What's going on?" I asked Thatcher quietly because I was sure someone had died or there was some other massive emergency.

"They know that we were faking it," he told me. "They know we were faking being together and they're kind of pissed at us for lying."

I swallowed hard.

"You told them?" I asked him, anger boiling my blood. Not specifically at him, but at the situation. Early on, he'd wanted to tell them the truth and so had I, but I was the one who'd stopped him. So most of that was probably directed at myself.

"Me?" His tone was one of outrage. "I didn't tell

them shit. Well, I guess I confirmed it, but they didn't find out from me."

I threw my hands in the air out of sheer frustration. "Who then? Who could've told them? We were the only ones who knew."

"Margot knew," he spat.

I winced. "She wouldn't tell anyone and she doesn't know any of them."

"Why'd you lie?" Lilah asked. "We're friends, right? Why didn't you just trust us?'

I took a deep breath and blew it out. I was terrible with confrontation due to years of being overpowered by the men in my life. I'd had few close friends and usually, we'd just grown apart without any fuss. I might've preferred it that way.

Now this was different.

"I couldn't risk my agent finding out."

"So those pictures were fake, too?" Charlotte asked.

"No." I sighed. "They, unfortunately, were real."

"Unfortunately," Thatcher muttered. Then he snorted.

"What I mean," I told them, "is those pictures were real. Yes, Thatcher offered to pretend to be my boyfriend, but we did not stage those pictures."

I turned to him for help, but it was clear in the

way he was leaning against the wall as if he didn't have a care in the world that he wasn't going to help me explain. He'd probably already been doing that before I got in here. But this was about my friendship with the girls so I had to be the one to handle it.

Everyone was angry that we'd lied to them. Not just at me, but at him too and it was weird to see the physical divide in the room.

But they'd get over it with him. He was their family and an important part of the band. On the other hand, I wasn't anybody to them other than a new friend who'd kept them in the dark.

"I'm sorry," I told them. "It was the only way I knew for sure it wouldn't get back to my agent."

"It's still a shitty thing to do," Charlotte told me and that one stung.

It *had* been a shitty thing to do. Once I'd gotten to know them, I should've insisted we tell them. Not doing so also put Thatcher in a bad position. At this moment, Sean came into the room. After looking around, he focused on Thatcher.

"I got that information you wanted." Sean glanced at me and then back to them as I waited to hear what they were talking about. My gut said it had something to do with me.

"Let's go," Thatcher replied, grabbing my arm to lead me from the room.

I snapped my arm out of his tight grip. "You don't need to manhandle me and I'd rather talk this through with them."

"We'll do that later. They'll get over it."

The girls' mouths dropped open at his assumption, but apparently, whatever he had going on was more important. To him. Not to me.

The three of us came to a stop in the hallway just outside the dressing room and it seemed like I was the only one in the dark.

"What'd you find out?" Thatcher asked.

Sean glanced uncomfortably at me. "They say it was her." And there was no doubt who the *her* was in this situation.

"Are they sure?"

Sean nodded as he tapped on his phone. "I just sent you the emails between us. There are screenshots."

Thatcher turned to me with a set jaw and anger burning his eyes. "Come on." He grabbed my arm again, but as I did before, I pulled it quickly back.

"What's going on?" I asked him, silently refusing to move another inch if he didn't tell me what he'd been talking to Sean about.

"You want to do this here?" He nodded. "OK. Why'd you have those pictures taken of us in the hot tub?"

"*What?*" I snapped back, like he'd slapped me because his words felt exactly like that.

"Listen, I don't really care what's out there about me, but that's a fucking invasion of privacy not to ask me first."

I began blinking rapidly as I didn't understand what he was saying. The words made sense individually, but all together in that order... not so much. "What?"

His jaw clenched and he rolled his eyes like I was the one being dense here but he hadn't told me anything yet. "Can we please go somewhere else to talk so we don't have a fucking audience?"

Nodding, I turned toward the venue exit. Thatcher didn't grab my arm this time. Instead, he flung his hand out in the international, silent way of saying *you first.*

Outside, he told me, "Bus."

So I guessed we were at one-word responses. But he seemed angry at me and I was so confused as to why. The closer we got to the bus, the more crushing the pain in my chest became.

In my life, it was normal for my father or Brian to

be angry with me. Once in a while, a director would get annoyed, especially when you were a kid just doing the best you could. It wasn't what the adults would have done and that irritated them.

However, I'd never had a friend mad at me and since I'd never had an actual boyfriend, one of those had never been mad at me. In my world, if someone thought you'd wronged them or they were pissed, outside of work, that was it. The relationship ended.

I didn't want that with Thatcher but was quickly accepting that our relationship was headed there. A breakup. My first. Deep down, I'd thought it would have lasted longer.

On the bus, Thatcher closed the door behind us then turned to me. "Tell me why you did it and tell me why you lied about it."

"We don't have to do this, Thatcher. I can just pack my things." In the movies, when there was a breakup, people said a lot of ugly things and anything remotely like that was the last thing I wanted to hear out of his mouth. "I just don't know what you're talking about."

If my dad telling me that all I'd be good for was porn had hurt, then something much less out of Thatcher would've devastated me.

"I just want to understand what happened."

"Well, I'd like to understand what you're talking about. You mentioned the pictures? You think I leaked them?"

Thatcher rubbed at his temple then took a deep breath. "I asked Sean to see if he could find out who sold those pictures to the site. He reached out and they said it was you. They have screenshots of your conversation, Modestie."

"What?" I whispered as he pulled his phone out of his pocket and brought up the offending pictures. "That's my number." He was telling the truth. The conversation between Sean and the site, the site and apparently me, was right there in front of my face.

According to the owner of the website, I admitted to hiring a paparazzi to take those pictures, told them when and where I'd be, then had them sell everything to the tabloid site.

Which was ridiculous. I hadn't done any of that. Yet the evidence said I had.

"So again, I ask why. Because I don't care what's out there about me." His hand hit his chest on the word *me*. "But I've been working hard to get to the bottom of this for you. Because you were so fucking upset. And you had those calls with your dad and agent. Was it so that you could finally fire him because you were too scared to do it otherwise?"

As I'd thought. The simplest thing from Thatcher was like stabbing me in the heart.

"I didn't do any of that, Thatcher," I said calmly. "I didn't even know we were going to the hot tub. That was your idea. Why were you trying to find out who did this? Why did it matter?"

"Because it fucking hurt you, Modestie," he yelled, causing me to take a step back. "It hurt you and I wanted to make it right. Somehow. I didn't know how. Maybe have a chat with the guy. Honestly, I was worried it was the fucking director and him, I've already been dying to talk to alone."

I shook my head. "That's why I didn't tell you about the emails." And there had been more than one, but Margot had been filtering them out for me. It wasn't until I'd gone looking that I'd seen the one I'd read hadn't been the only one.

He cocked his head to the side. "Emails?"

After swallowing hard, I shook my head. "Nothing. Never mind."

"What emails, Modestie?"

"They're nothing. But you get so angry that I chose not to tell you." Which wasn't exactly the truth. I hadn't told him because I hadn't wanted to bother him. He had a lot on his plate without my drama. I was trying to be as drama-free as I could be, given that he hadn't even been my real boyfriend at the time.

"So, more lying?"

"I didn't lie," I told him. He raised an eyebrow because clearly, we had lied to the band about us.

"What else?" he asked, coming closer to be but still speaking far too loud so that I knew he was angry. "What else aren't you telling me?"

"Nothing." But there was more. "I received an offer for a streaming series. A limited series, actually, I think." The official offer had come in this morning without me even needing to read for the part, and at first, I'd been going to reject it, but right now that seemed like a bad idea. It'd give me a reason, an excuse to leave the tour so he could calm down.

"What?"

"On my first call with my new agent, she said she had a streaming series that might be perfect for me. Only ten episodes, so it wouldn't eat up my entire year but multiple seasons of it. I'd have time to do the Lucas project. But I'd have to be in L.A. pretty immediately to get started on pre-production."

His jaw turned to granite, only now he took two steps away from me. "So... you decided we should lie to the band and your new friends, you get pictures of us plastered on the internet in a very fucking intimate moment, you've been receiving emails from a man obsessed with fucking you and didn't tell me, plus, you're thinking about taking a series that means you leave right away and didn't want to discuss it with me." He held his arms out in front of him. "Anything else? Were you honest about *anything*?"

I snapped back again because when he laid it all out like that, it did sound like I'd been doing exactly what he was accusing me of.

Had I?

Not intentionally.

"I don't know how the photos happened, Thatcher. I don't. They hurt me far worse than they hurt you and I didn't do that. I don't know why those screenshots show it coming from my email. I don't." I took a deep breath because I wasn't sure he believed me. "I'm going to take the series," I said impulsively. It hadn't been a decision that I'd even thought I'd make, but now... it seemed like the best one.

It'd remove me, the problem, from the equation. I'd be working, which meant I'd be happy. Thatcher could return to his pre-Modestie life. My heart was breaking but it seemed like the best option.

But Thatcher shook his head. "We should talk about that because you know we don't do well long-distance. We didn't before. It's one thing to be gone a few months filming but another to spend half the year apart or what the fuck ever."

"We were always going to be long-distance," I told him because it was true. Eventually, I'd be filming and he'd be on the road. Or he'd be at home and I'd be in another country. Nothing about our situation had really changed since we'd been teenagers. Except for the fact that we both had the money to make trips back and forth.

"For short periods, Modestie." He sighed heavily. "Not like this. "You're taking a streaming series that films for how long? Will it have multiple seasons? You said you think but you don't know. We need to talk about these things. I can come to you some of the time but..." He blew out a breath. "We need to figure it out before you decide."

I didn't answer him and didn't correct him. Yes, shows were normally filmed for long periods of time, but this wasn't like that. It was only ten episodes, which meant shooting took less time. But maybe Thatcher was right about me hiding things because that was the first thing I thought to do about... well, everything.

Thatcher stormed over to me and leaned down so that we were eye to eye. "If you leave right now, I'm worried it'll be over."

My heart thudded against my ribs, like it was trying to stop me from doing something stupid, but this wasn't that. It'd break my heart, sure, but that would be something I'd have to heal from.

For now, given that I was apparently the cause of all of this, it was better for me to leave. "Did we ever even get started?"

His eyebrows shot up as he stood to his full height. "I thought we had. My mistake. If you want to leave, pack your shit and don't be here after the show."

He left the bus with the slam of the door that shook the entire thing.

I swallowed hard and hurried to pack my things up while trying not to sob like a crazy person.

All of this was bad, but the worst was that I didn't even have anyone here to say goodbye to.

19

THATCHER

Everything inside me screamed to go back into the bus for Modestie. But I couldn't keep her there if she didn't want to be there.

She'd said she was taking the streaming job, causing something inside me to snap.

She was the entire fucking reason that I didn't do relationships. I'd wanted her in high school and couldn't have her, other than for that one night. If I couldn't have her, I didn't want anyone else.

So I'd avoided getting emotionally attached to anyone since and that had worked just fine. Then she blew back into my life and it was like a one-two punch. She'd had my heart before I'd seen her that day at the premiere. Fuck, for all I knew, she'd seen me there and planned the whole thing to get me all tied up in her.

Even I didn't believe that. I was just being an asshole even if no one else could hear it. She'd been scared when that fucker had her backed into the corner and while she might've been a fantastic actress, she hadn't known anyone was watching.

Fuck. I'd been upset when Modestie had come into the dressing room because everyone had been pissed and were on me about not telling them that we were pretending. All because Lilah overheard Modestie on the phone with Margot. But this had gone off the rails and we both needed to calm down.

Besides, I had to do the fucking soundcheck.

"What happened?" London asked when I got back into the dressing room.

"Nothing."

"Doesn't look like nothing," Grayson told me.

The women were off to the side near the clothes that Lilah and Becca were setting up, acting like they couldn't hear every word out of our mouths.

"Yeah. You're right." I sighed as I ran a hand through my hair. "Sean found out that Modestie was the one to sell those pictures to the website. That she set it up."

"That doesn't make any sense." Grayson folded

his arms over his chest. "She'd been upset by those, right?'

I nodded. "And saying it out loud, I know how fucked-up it was that I even considered she'd do something like that. But it was like all the lies piled up." I scrubbed a hand through my hair. "Fuck. It was probably her dad or that fucking agent."

"So were you faking it the whole time?" Jamison asked, which of course he would.

I shook my head. "I wasn't faking it at all. Or it was supposed to be in the beginning but I only made the offer because I've had it bad for her since high school."

He clapped loudly. "I knew it." Like that was some sort of victory for him. "I knew you were into her as more than friends. I can see through bullshit."

"Yeah. Congratulations." I threw my hands out to the side. "It's all fucked now."

"What do you mean 'the lies piling up'?" Lennox was the one to bring us back to the topic at hand.

I let myself fall back against the wall not far from where I'd been when Modestie had come in. There was no reason not to tell them. "Lying to all of you about our relationship, which I'm fucking sorry about."

"We don't care," they all said at the same time.

"But they do." I nodded toward the women on the other side of the room.

"They'll calm down," Grayson assured me, but it didn't work.

"Anyway, lying about the relationship after we decided to tell you which, by the way, we did come to tell you almost at the beginning. We had said we were going to be honest with you all at the beginning but then she freaked about it getting back to her agent. Then when we weren't faking anymore we should've told you then. Lying about her feelings for me, obviously, which I did too. Lying about the pictures, which I now don't even think she did but when I was with her on the bus, I did think that and that's so far beyond fucked up, I'm embarrassed of myself." I took a quick breath and swallowed all of my anger at myself for now. "Then apparently, she's been getting emails from that fucking director and never said a word. For a split second, it made me wonder if she lied about the phone calls from her dad and agent."

"She didn't," Avalon said quickly.

I looked up to see Avalon headed our way. "How do you know? You saw her crying. She told you it was them but how do you know?"

"I was there, remember? She had her phone on

speaker. I heard every nasty word. Now, I didn't understand her conversation with her father, but the look on her face was enough. That really happened too."

Charlotte raised her hand in the air. "I was there too. Well, not for the last part because I came to find you, but the way her agent spoke to her... It really was disgusting."

"He probably set the whole thing up with pics," Jamison told me and once he'd said it, it was obvious. "Him or that fucking director. What's his deal anyway? It's not hard to make an email address that looks like it's from someone."

"He's hellbent on fucking her." There wasn't a better way of saying that. "Apparently. And he's wanted her since she was seventeen."

"So he's more than a creeper." Lennox said what we were all thinking. Modestie had been seventeen, but Brecht had been a grown-ass adult trying to use his power over her. "She's probably the first to say *no* and that's why he can't let it go."

"Maybe."

"We heard what was in the email," Avalon offered and now it was the only thing I could focus on. She turned to Charlotte. "Remember?"

"Yes." Charlotte nodded. "She gave us a rundown but didn't read it to us."

"Right," Avalon agreed. "She said that he wanted her in the movie, but they could use a body double for the nude scenes. He also said that he wanted to make sure she could really see his vision and they could go through the scene in private. Or something like that. It was clearly a ploy to get her naked and alone."

The red-hot rage I felt when it came to the guy wasn't like anything I'd ever experienced before. And to think he'd been doing this to other women for lord-knew-how-long. And now I'd just sent her out into the fucking world alone to face that motherfucker.

The full significance of what I'd done in that argument with Modestie settled in, causing me to sigh with frustration at myself.

Let's be honest. I had no idea what I was doing in a relationship, given that I'd avoided them my entire adult life.

Because of her.

Because she was the only one I wanted to be with for longer than one night and I couldn't have her then. I had her now and I'd just shit the bed.

"I have to go talk to her," I told them, knowing

that they'd understand. Before I could even get out the door, Sean came in and I knew I wasn't going to like what he had to say.

"Where are you headed?" he asked me. There must've been determination all over my face because he furrowed his brows.

"I have to go talk to Modestie."

He shook his head as he said, "She'll have to wait. We have to hop on a call with the label."

"Can't they do it without me?"

He cocked his head to the side and narrowed his eyes. "Are you part of this band?" I didn't answer because we all knew that I was. "We can't make these decisions without you. You can skip sound-check, though."

I gritted my teeth together. He was right. When it came to decisions, we all needed to be there.

It was the longest twenty minutes of my life and I couldn't focus on what we were discussing with the label execs. As soon as Sean hung up, I sprinted from the room. Any follow-up could wait.

I hurried past everyone in the hallway, most of who stopped to stare like they were going to see something interesting instead of me as a blur as I dashed away from them. I didn't slow down when I plowed through the door. I'd left her on the bus, so I figured that was where she'd still be.

"Modestie," I called out. There was no answer.

I tore through that bus, pulling back curtains and checking the back room. When I pulled back the curtain in front of where we kept our things, I found all of her stuff gone. There were no clothes. No suitcase.

Fuck. She was gone.

Pulling my phone out of my pocket, I chose her contact as quickly as I could.

It rang three times as I squeezed my phone so hard, I thought I might break.

"Modestie Dubois' phone." That wasn't her voice and there was only one person I could think of who would answer her phone.

"Margot?"

"Speaking." She had to know it was me, right? But she acted like she didn't. Did Modestie delete me from her phone already so that my name and picture didn't come up when I called?

"It's Thatcher. Let me talk to Modestie."

"Oh, no can do." She didn't sound the least bit upset by that.

"Listen, Margot, I have to talk to her. How is she in L.A. already?"

"She's not." Something cracked in the background, but I couldn't tell if it was a chair or a door or what. At this point, I couldn't have cared less.

"What?"

Margot sighed like I was an annoyance taking time out of her day. "She's not here. She forwarded her phone to me so anyone who might call her would get me. I wonder why she would do that." Again, her tone said she already knew all about it.

"I fucked up."

"Yeah, you did and it's really disappointing." No shit. "I was rooting for you, Thatcher. I was hoping the whole fake thing would turn out to be real because I haven't seen Modestie as relaxed as she was with you. Ever. And I'm talking *ever*."

I pulled the phone away from my ear and fought the urge to throw it before bringing it back in. "Where is she?"

"I'm not supposed to tell you, but..." There was a momentary pause that I thought would kill me. "You know what? No. I can't tell you that without her permission and she explicitly told me not to and since she's my friend as well as my boss, I'm going to listen to her."

"Margot," I snapped.

"No can do, Thatcher. She doesn't want you

calling her. Respect her wishes. I will tell her you called though."

Then the call ended.

Fucking hell.

Of course I wanted to respect Modestie's wishes, but if those wishes meant that I'd never get to apologize, I didn't think I could do it. So how was I supposed to do both?

With my shoulders slumping and feeling like I'd just been sucker-punched in the heart, I headed back into the venue. There was nothing else I could do right now and that pissed me off even more.

"Did you talk to her?" London asked as soon as I got back to the dressing room. I could only shake my head.

Grayson came forward and asked, "Where is she?"

"Gone," I told him. "Because of my dumb ass, she's gone."

"Go after her," Avalon told me like I hadn't already thought of that.

"Go where?" I threw my hands in the air helplessly. "I have no fucking clue where she is. I called, but her phone has been forwarded to Margot."

"Wow," Lilah said quietly like she didn't think I'd hear her. "She really cut him out."

She wasn't even talking to me, but out of instinct, I marched toward her, stopping after three steps. "I fucking know that. I really don't need you telling me that."

Grayson hopped in front of me. "Bring it back down, brother, because if you keep yelling at my girlfriend, then you and I are going to have a problem."

"I'm sorry," I told her. "I'm not yelling at you. I'm yelling at myself."

"I know that," she told me. "Thank you for apologizing."

"I don't know what the fuck to do."

"Where would she go?" Charlotte asked.

"I assume the airport." Because she probably wanted to get as far away from my dumb ass as possible. "But there's no way for me to get there and find her. Is she headed to L.A.? No fucking clue. Paris? Some fucking tiny island I've never heard of? Her options and money are endless."

The fact that Modestie had unlimited amounts of money at her disposal made this harder. She literally could've been going anywhere on this planet. Fuck, for all I know she could be headed off the planet. She had the money to do it.

"You'll have to keep trying." Avalon wrapped her arms around her stomach.

I narrowed my eyes on the group of women in our dressing room. They were always fucking there and knew just about everything. "Aren't you all still pissed at her? You all started this in the first place."

"Whoa." Avalon held her hand up to make sure I knew that I'd crossed a line. It made sense for her to be their spokesperson, given that she'd known all of us forever. "We are angry, as we have the right to be when someone breaks our trust. That doesn't mean that we didn't want her here anymore."

"She lied."

Avalon cocked her head to the side and narrowed her eyes. "So did you. Yet you're still here." She quickly wet her lips then crossed the room so she was closer to me. "We were upset because we got emotionally invested in her, in your relationship. To find out you'd been lying the entire time..." She shook her head. "That hurt. We would've worked through it if you hadn't decided she was lying about everything she's ever said and made her feel that way."

"I have a thought." Charlotte stepped forward with her finger in the air before dropping it, breaking a tiny bit of the tension that had formed in the room. "From the things we've talked about, it didn't sound like Modestie has ever had too many people in her corner. Her father's trash, clearly. Her agent was in cahoots with her father. She never mentioned a past relationship or a close friend except Margot, who also works for her, and her costar, Evan, who she's still close with."

"What's your point?" I asked, trying not to sound as irritated as I felt so that Lennox wouldn't be on my ass, too.

"That maybe she's never had an argument with her friend or boyfriend. Maybe she thought an argument means it's over. Plus, you were a dick, and while it wouldn't shock the rest of us that you guys can be dicks, maybe it did her. You've probably never been a dick to her."

Suddenly, Lilah was right there next to Avalon. "I agree. Leaving like that isn't necessarily a normal response, is it?"

I clenched my jaw. "I don't know, Lilah. What would you do if Grayson accused you of lying about everything? Or if he said that you'd be over if you had to do long-distance?"

She winced. "You said that?"

I didn't answer because I didn't need to. I'd asked the questions, which was basically the same thing.

Jamison smacked his hands together then rubbed them like he was warming them over a fire. "There's good news." I doubted it. "We have a show to do tonight and that should be enough to get your mind off any woman. Even a sexy mega superstar."

He was wrong. Dead wrong.

I'd play tonight because I had to and I couldn't run around the world trying to find the woman I loved. If I had any idea where she was, that was where I'd be, begging for her to talk to me, to let me apologize.

Instead, I had to play and wait until she either answered her phone or Margot caved.

If I would've known how long that would take, I probably would've gone insane that night.

20

MODESTIE

I had never packed and left anywhere as quickly as I did that bus. How everything was packed meant nothing to me. All I knew is that I could never face any of them again after that. The quick friendship as well as any hope of a relationship with Thatcher was over.

Margot had told me he'd called while I'd still been on my way to the airport, but I'd held firm. No information went to Thatcher.

In my world, once you had an argument, it was over. No one had ever tried to work things out like that with me. When I made a mistake, I lost people. Not that I had many people in the first place. Now, you could wait until it completely imploded or you could walk away. The only time it hadn't been true was when it came to Brian or my father. They stayed because I was their payday.

Even they were both gone now.

I had Margot and I had Gabrielle, my new agent. Who, by the way, had gone right to work for me.

After leaving Thatcher, I went to hide out in New York for a few days. Margot had offered to meet me, but I wanted to be alone.

This broken heart was so much worse than it had been when I'd been seventeen. Back then, I'd known there was no chance of being with Thatcher. Now, I'd had hope, and losing hope was the most painful of all.

After four days, I grabbed a plane back to L.A., hoping that I wouldn't get recognized along the way. I didn't really think Thatcher would be following gossip sites that report celebrity sightings, but if he did, he'd know where I was.

Who was I kidding? He wasn't looking.

He'd called once, I figured because he'd felt like he had to, and that was it.

Time to move on.

"So, you like this one?" Margot asked after we looked at the second house she'd chosen for me.

"It's great. I really don't care, if I'm being honest. Maybe I should just go home."

"Home? Modestie, this is also your home."

I shrugged. She wasn't wrong. "I meant Paris. I haven't been there in a while."

"No way." We walked back out to the foyer. "You're finally getting everything you want. You're not running off because of some man. You need to be here to get some projects lined up." She held her hand up to stop me from speaking before I even started. "Yes, I know you can do that from anywhere, but you're just cultivating your relationship with Gabrielle. You need to be here. So..." She took a step back and held her arms up. "How about this one?"

I looked around the house one more time and if I were being honest, it was my favorite of the ones she'd shown me. This was only the second that I'd checked out in person, but I'd seen more pictures than I cared to admit.

I'd told Thatcher I was taking the series because it was an easy excuse to leave but I decided not to do it when I was in New York. It wasn't what I wanted yet.

This house was large, but not multi-million dollar, felt-too-big-for-one-person large. There were four bedrooms, five bathrooms, plenty of space for if Margot stayed here sometimes. A pool, which I could see myself sitting beside reading scripts while enjoying the warm air.

This was as good as any.

"Yes. I think this one will do."

"Excellent." She tapped on her iPad, probably sending the real estate agent a message as we spoke. The agent had been here, but Margot had insisted that we'd needed time alone and I was a celebrity. They weren't going to turn her down.

The idea of living alone didn't bother me. I'd done that most of my life. Even before I'd started acting, I'd had a nanny. No, I hadn't technically been alone, but I may as well have been.

"OK." She sighed. "She's going to put in an offer, see what negotiation needs to take place, and get this baby purchased ASAP."

"Thank you, Margot." I gave her a quick hug.

"Hey. It's my job." She led me to the front door that she promised to lock behind us. "Now, let's get some food."

I wasn't hungry, but I went along with it anyway. We chose my favorite mom-and-pop place that was out of the way but had great food. No one tended to bug anyone else there and it was off the beaten path, so anyone looking for a celebrity encounter would be far away.

We chose to sit outside on their patio because it was such a beautiful day. Then we ordered a plate of tacos to share as well as drinks.

While we waited for the food, Margot twisted her napkin in her hands over and over before putting it down and taking a deep breath. "I have some news."

"News?" I raised an eyebrow but fought back the hope that it was about Thatcher. I hadn't transferred my calls back to my own phone yet, but she would've told me if he'd been calling. And it'd been two weeks. Hope shouldn't even have been on my radar.

She nodded. "Gabrielle and I have been looking into those photos because we both know you didn't send them to the website."

"Of course I didn't."

"Well, we got to the bottom of it and it was Brian."

I sat up straighter. "What?"

She nodded again and wet her bottom lip. "Yeah. My guess is he thought if you were exposed, he and your dad would give you a hard time, then you'd cave and do Brecht's movie."

"But... what? How?"

She shrugged. "I heard it's easy to spoof a phone number, but since he had access to everything of yours through your dad, my guess is they cloned your phone so it'd look like it was coming from you. I'm not an expert though."

"We've locked them out of everything, right?" I asked. She nodded. "Good. I want to get a new phone then too."

She hurriedly started tapping on the iPad. "Got it. New number, too?"

I almost said *yes* without thinking about it, but if I changed my phone number, there were people who wouldn't be able to get a hold of me if they ever wanted to.

And there was that damned hope again.

"Not yet. Just the new phone."

"Got it."

"Why would he do that?" I asked, not thinking she'd have the answer. "I mean, I understand that it was part of a plan to convince me to get naked on screen, but why did he care so much?"

"Apparently, Brecht was going to give Brian a huge reward for convincing you. Then Brian would give some of that to your dad. So they had a vested interest. It wouldn't have been difficult to find out where you were with your credit cards and things like that."

"Listen, I know my breasts are amazing, but

Jesus-fucking-Christ, are they really worth all of *that*?"

Margot snickered but covered it with her hand. "I guess they are."

Our food arrived and we dove in, letting all the delicious spices marinate in our mouths. This little place had been our secret place for a couple of years. It was where we went to eat whenever we needed cheering up.

I wasn't very hungry but I still munched and as I ate, I realized I did really need sustenance.

"Can I ask you something?" She'd just finished her first taco and I was about to.

"Go ahead." Though I was worried about what she wanted to ask, given she'd never needed permission to say anything to me before.

"Why did you leave without talking it out?"

I didn't have to think about what she was talking about. The question was: Did I want to explain? I couldn't chance an argument with Margot, too. I'd be lost without her.

"He said ugly things—"

"You told me."

"So I didn't think he'd want me there when he got back. He'd already made it clear that we weren't going to work since we'd have to be apart a lot, so why wait? Just leave."

"Yeah, but you made friends on that tour. What about them?"

I swallowed the bite I'd just taken hard. "That was done too. They'd have to take his side and honestly if you argue with someone other than Brian or my father, they tend to not speak to you again."

She furrowed her brows. "Man, this industry has fucked with your head."

"What?"

"You haven't had a single healthy relationship with anyone except Thatcher and the guys in high school, which ended because of distance; Evan, who you're still close with, but you two can not talk for months then pick up like no time had passed." That part was true. "And then me. But you've never had like a super close friend, or a boyfriend, who wasn't fucked up."

"I've never had a boyfriend, unless you count Thatcher for those couple of days or whatever it was after he told me that he loved me. Before that it was just the guy I sometimes had mediocre sex with."

"That's my point. You don't trust people."

My lips parted in surprise. "I trust *you*."

"I work for you. You could fire me at any

moment. I mean, personal trust. You've been trained by your trash-ass father that you can't trust anyone."

Slowly, I set my second taco on my plate and wiped my hands on the napkin while I thought about what she'd said.

She was right. I didn't trust people to be there for me unless I paid them to be. Margot was my friend, yes, but maybe that was why I only felt comfortable having a friend I paid. She *had to* be there.

With the girls on the tour, them getting mad at me meant we weren't friends anymore because it never occurred to me that it could be another way.

The same was true about my relationship with Thatcher. We'd been close while I'd been at school, but we'd all known that had an expiration date. We didn't have to have a falling out because I'd been leaving. It had been easy when it had been fake because there'd been expectations that wouldn't be met. Loving him from a distance was easy.

It was safe.

"Are you trying to tell me that all of that was just a minor argument and we could've worked it out?" I asked.

She set her own taco on her plate and leaned over the table. "I don't *know* if you could've worked it out, but I know you couldn't if you didn't talk to him after."

I dropped my head into my hands while fighting tears. I hadn't cried over Thatcher or the whole situation since my first day in New York. I wouldn't let myself. I'd pushed all those feelings into a box in the corner of my heart and wouldn't let them out.

Now that box was opening itself, exploding all over me like there was a gremlin inside trying to get out.

"Hey." Margot was suddenly beside me with her arm around my shoulders as she rubbed my arm. "It's not your fault your father fucked you up. It can be fixed."

"It can't be fixed." I looked up at her with burning eyes. "I left. I cut them all off. My phone still goes to yours after two weeks. That's a pretty clear message."

"You're in luck," she told me. "Your guy is in a band that is currently on tour. Which means we know where he'll be. We can fix this if you want it to be fixed."

I nodded as a tear rolled down my cheek. "I told him I was taking the streaming series."

She snorted. "He believed you? You're not doing streaming just yet. That's not part of the plan."

"I know. I knew then, too, but I still said it."

"Oh, honey…" She brought me in for a hug. "That was a defense mechanism, I'm sure. Maybe you need therapy. But what do you need *right now?*"

"I need to figure out where he is and talk to him."

"Good thing you have me."

The next day, I was climbing into a car service Margot hired for me in Louisville, Kentucky, to take me to the arena where Forever 18 was playing. No one knew I was coming and I'd never been so nervous to do anything in my life.

I'd only brought a small bag with me because I honestly didn't think I'd be staying long enough to need more and if I did, I'd go shopping. Margot had gotten the new phone for me and set it up and we'd transferred calls back to my phone. The only person I'd contacted so far was Margot because she'd insisted on knowing that I was OK.

When I arrived, there were already fans outside. Fans who couldn't care less that I was there and for that, I was thankful. Security stopped me, but I still had my all access tour pass from when I'd been on the tour, and imagine my surprise when I found out that he didn't laugh in my face.

He stepped aside so I could get by him.

I'd never been to this venue before, but I used

what I'd learned on tour to find the back entrance and get inside. Dropping my bag by the door, I readied myself for a massive search for the dressing room. I'd worn a dress today. A mid-thigh-length sundress that swept against my legs as I walked and flattered my figure. My hair was down and I tossed my big sunglasses on top of the bag so that the only accessory I had on was my purse crossing my body.

Turned out, I didn't have to look that hard.

There was the noise of them coming down the hallway and it was all of them as far as I could tell. Perfect. Just what I didn't want. Getting Thatcher alone would've been better, but I wasn't turning back. I'd come here to talk to him and that was what I was going to do.

"Oh, wow," Avalon said as she stopped short after being the first person to notice me standing there.

That brought everyone's attention right to me.

Thatcher's jaw tightened and he pushed his hands into his pockets. Before I had a chance to say anything, the rest of the band and the girls got moving again, which would leave the two of us alone. As she passed, Charlotte gave my arm a squeeze in a move that I thought was meant to reassure me.

Then it was just the two of us. There weren't even workers in this part of the hallway.

He waited, but when I didn't speak, he raised his eyebrows. "What're you doing here, Modestie?"

"I came to talk to you."

He shook his head. "I tried to talk to you two weeks ago. What's changed?"

I took a deep breath. "Is there somewhere we could talk alone?"

"We *are* alone," he countered and he wasn't wrong. We were alone, but I meant where someone wouldn't be able to happen upon us.

"OK." I blew out a breath willing my stomach to stop tumbling over itself. "I'm sorry I left like I did. I should've stayed to talk to you. To work things out." I swallowed hard. "Margot figured out some things about me."

"Like what?"

"I don't know how relationships work." There was no other way to explain it.

"What?"

"In my life, anytime I had an argument with a friend, the relationship ended. It was either that or we just grew apart. They didn't even have to be friends. Co-stars, too."

"We weren't just *friends*, Modestie."

"I know." I fought the tears that were threatening to spill. I didn't want to go for sympathy with him. "But I've never had this kind of relationship. I've gone on dates. I had the one guy I sometimes had sex with. That's about it. Nothing solid. Nothing that lasted."

Thatcher sighed as he watched me intently.

I wanted him to reach out to me so badly and when he didn't, I thought for sure this wasn't good enough.

Everything I wanted was right there in front of me yet just out of reach.

21

THATCHER

I'd wanted Modestie to be standing in front of me for two weeks. I'd called but had listened to Margot about respecting her wishes. I'd composed a hundred texts not caring that she wouldn't see them but never sent a single one.

Now she was standing in front of me and I had to fight all of my urges. There were many.

I wanted to yell at her for leaving. Hug her because she was back. Fuck some sense into her. Tell her it was too late. Tell her I needed her to be mine.

I wasn't going to do any of those things.

"Come on," I told her as I turned around and walked away.

The guys were all going out for food, so the

dressing room was going to be deserted. That was where I took her.

Modestie didn't move to sit on one of the seats, so I didn't, either. I leaned against the back of the couch that was in the middle of the room. She came closer, but not so close that I could reach out and touch her if I wanted to. Who was I kidding? I fucking wanted to.

"You were saying?" I asked.

"That was about it. I'm not good with relationships. In my experience, other than my dad and Brian, people didn't talk after an argument. It didn't even have to be a big one. Most of the people I thought of as friends... we just grew apart. However, the ones where we'd have a disagreement, it was just over. No coming back from that."

"Who the fuck have you been hanging out with?"

She gave me a small grin. "No one good. I don't keep friends long, so when everyone was mad at me... I assumed that was how it was going to go and I bolted because it hurt so damn much." Her voice broke near the end of her sentence, which made my fingers itch to touch her.

"You can't do that," I told her because her taking off wasn't something I'd go through again.

"I know." Her voice was quiet... small.

"What do you want now, Modestie?"

She didn't hesitate to answer. "You. I want you. I wasn't lying when I said I love you. I wasn't actually lying about a lot of things but I never lied about you."

I ran a hand down my face in frustration because now it was my turn to get things out. "I know you weren't lying. We lied to everyone and they were upset. But they're our friends. Our family. They get over those things."

She snorted. "I don't have a great track record with family, either."

"I know." My thoughts darkened at what I'd like to do to her father for being the way he was with her. For teaching her that people only wanted something from her and showing her she couldn't trust anyone. "But it's different here, yeah?"

She bit her lips together and nodded.

"Come here," I said, quietly demanding that she do it.

Her breathing increased as she scurried over and stopped right before me. I pushed my fingers into her hair so that I could cradle her face. As she looked up at me with those beautiful coppery eyes, I knew I needed to speak before I did something else.

"I'm sorry that I said you lied about everything. I

know that's not exactly what happened, but I can't have you hiding anything from me. Emails from assholes included," I insisted. She nodded quickly. "No, baby. You have to tell me you understand."

"I understand," she said softly. I ran a thumb over her bottom lip.

"You had a lot going on and I didn't tell you because of it. Now I'll just add to your plate."

"You *are* my plate. Yeah, I care about other things, but you're the priority."

"I love you, Thatcher."

"I love you, too."

Another minute couldn't happen without me kissing her. As I pressed my lips to hers, her fingers circled my forearms, like she was trying to bring me closer. I might've wanted to be a lot fucking closer to her right now, but there were still things we had to discuss.

After ending the kiss, I remained close so that my lips could almost brush her skin as I spoke. "Are you mine? Do you want to be mine?"

She closed her eyes and leaned into my touch. "Yes."

"I'm yours too." I kissed her gently again. "How long can you stay?"

Her eyes popped open with excitement. "I won't

start filming the new movie for a few months. There will be some pre-production stuff I'll have to be there for, but I can fly out when that happens."

"What about the streaming series?"

Her face fell. "I lied. Or not really. I said I was taking it because at the time, I'd decided to. It was an excuse. A reason to leave." She shook her head softly. "I'm not taking the series."

"How about in the future, we talk to each other before freaking out? Because I've never done this relationship thing, either. We are going to stumble. We need to rely on each other to keep from falling."

"Absolutely. I won't run again. I'll tell you every time an email comes in."

I chuckled deeply in my chest. "I don't need to know every detail, Modestie. I just need to know when you receive any messages from a guy trying to fuck you who is also trying to intimidate you. Or from anyone who causes you a problem. Because it'd be my problem, too."

Her eyes grew wide. "I didn't send those pictures," she said. I furrowed my brows. "Margot and Gabrielle were able to find out that Brian cloned my phone and made it look like I did, but I didn't. I wouldn't."

"When I really thought about it, I knew you hadn't done it."

"So we're good?" There was so much hope in her eyes.

"We're good. We're better than good because I have at least ninety minutes in which I can take you back to the bus and show you how much I've missed you."

She giggled as her cheeks pinked up and I hoped that was something that would never go away because if I could spend the rest of my life making Modestie Dubois blush, then I'd die a happy man.

PREORDER NOW

If you're not quite ready to let go of Thatcher and Modesties, keep reading for an awesome BONUS SCENE! Enjoy!

BONUS SCENE

Dear Reader,

I hope you enjoyed Forever Thatcher. Thatcher & Modestie were so much fun for me and had me swooning. I'm excited for you to read more about them.

I have a bonus scene for you as a thank you for reading. Just click the link below, sign up for my newsletter, and you'll get an email with the bonus scene.

SIGN UP HERE:
https://geni.us/ThatcherBonus

FOREVER JAMISON

Forever 18 Book 5

BLURB COMING SOON

Get Forever Jamison now!

Love your rock stars? Check out…

Daisy

Pushing Daisies Book 1

Daisy's too young for Lawson. But that's not going to stop her.

Being in a band with my brothers isn't always easy but we just got our big break. Somehow, our manager snagged us the opening spot for Courting Chaos. Even with having to live on a bus for months with my four brothers, this is an opportunity of a lifetime.

Their manager, Lawson, is stupid hot but after witnessing me in an embarrassing situation, I know there's no hope of anything between us.

Grab Daisy today!

Still want more?

Cross

Courting Chaos Book 1

A sexy drummer and a rock god's daughter…what could possibly go wrong?

All I want is to spend a nice summer with my rock star father.

But then some random guy assumes I'm a groupie and tries to kick me out of the venue.

That's never happened before. Imagine my surprise

when I find out that the random guy is actually
Cross Rhodes, the smoking hot drummer for
Courting Chaos, Dad's opener.
I don't fall for rock stars—ever. Yet Cross quickly has
me wanting to break *all* the rules.

Grab Cross Today!

THE HARBOR POINT SERIES

A new adult contemporary romance series

Meet Gio and Sal.
Two damaged men who meet the woman who can
set them right.

Then there's Cash.
He's not damaged but he's ready to do the healing
when he meets Gemma.

Check out the Harbor Point Series today!

THE FALLOUT SERIES

A new adult romance series

Coming home is hard.
Finding out the boy you loved had a baby with your
former best friend... heartbreaking.

Check out The Fallout Series today!

GAMBLING ON LOVE

A new adult romance series

Desperate times call for desperate measures so Flannery Tate is selling her virginity.

Check out Gambling on Love today!

I you'd like to just keep up with my sales and new releases, you can follow me on BookBub!

Bookbub: https://www.bookbub.com/authors/ heather-young-nichols

About the Author

Heather Young-Nichols is a USA Today Bestselling author of contemporary and paranormal romance. A native of the great and often very cold state of Michigan, she is better known at home and to her friends as the Snarker-in-Chief. A job she excels at beyond anything she could have imagined. She loves many things, but especially cold coffee, hot books, and baseball. But not necessarily in that order.

Find Heather on Social Media or by visiting her website.

heatheryoungnichols.com

facebook.com/heatheryoungnicholsauthor

instagram.com/heatheryoungnichols

amazon.com/Heather-Young-Nichols/e/B00KKTM54A

bookbub.com/authors/heather-young-nichols

tiktok.com/@heatheryoungnichols